Rimrock Renegade

Ned Oaks

A Black Horse Western

ROBERT HALE

© Ned Oaks 2016
First published in Great Britain 2016

ISBN 978-0-7198-2036-6

The Crowood Press
The Stable Block
Crowood Lane
Ramsbury
Marlborough
Wiltshire SN8 2HR

www.crowood.com

Robert Hale is an imprint
of The Crowood Press

Derek Doyle & Associates, Shaw Heath
Printed and bound in Great Britain by
CPI Group (UK) Ltd, Croydon, CR0 4YY

Rimrock Renegade

Hank Chesham spent five years in a New Mexico prison, convicted of a crime he didn't commit. When he was finally released, he only wanted to return home to his ranch, the Rimrock, and resume his old life. But then he discovered that he had been betrayed by both his wife, Phoebe, and his best friend, Ted Flynn, who had conspired to steal the Rimrock from him.

Now Chesham has but one thing on his mind: vengeance. Before he can take action, however, Flynn unleashes some of his hired killers and nearly succeeds in eliminating the Rimrock's real owner. Chesham barely survives after he is secretly nursed back to health by his former wife's sister, Mandy. They decide to make a future together.

Back in fighting shape, Chesham takes on Ted Flynn, and he will stop at nothing until he brings his enemies to their knees and reclaims what is rightfully his.

PROLOGUE

New Mexico, 1882

Pile Territorial Penitentiary was located in the desert about ten miles south of Santa Fe. It had been named for William Anderson Pile, a Republican governor appointed by President Grant. However, for the prisoners who lived within its walls, 'pile' had connotations completely unrelated to politics.

'The Pile' is what they called it. Many of the guards did, too, although the warden disapproved. It was, by any measure, the worst prison in the arid Southwest. Given the general state of prisons in New Mexico, Arizona, Nevada, and California, that was no small feat.

Some areas of the Pile were nicer than others. The cell where they held Hank Chesham in solitary confinement was the worst to be found in the brick and adobe structure. Many men who had been sent into that cell alive had come out dead.

The cell was on the back corner of the top floor of the main prison block. There was no relief from the molten heat in the daytime, and at night it got so cold that Chesham invariably curled into a shivering ball, teeth chattering. His bed was a pile of smelly straw, and he hadn't been provided with a blanket. He had been in the cell, alternately roasting and freezing, for over a month now. All because he had defended himself from a mad man who had been hell bent on killing him.

Chesham had been in the Pile for nearly five years. He had been convicted of robbing a stage coach and, despite protesting his innocence, sentenced to twenty years in prison. From the day he had been transferred from the jail in Santa Fe, he had known to be on his guard. The Pile was a very dangerous place, and any sign of weakness would be exploited by the other prisoners, or the guards.

Chesham was a loner. He hadn't made friends with the other prisoners, and he hadn't tried to curry favor with the violent thugs who ruled the cell blocks. He despised them, although he had never tried to provoke conflict with them. And he didn't fear them – which made them hate him. Butch Tancred was the most powerful and vicious prisoner in the Pile, and he had decided to teach Chesham a lesson.

When Tancred had demanded that Chesham take another prisoner's place on laundry duty, Chesham had refused. After that, he was a marked man. He knew it, and everyone else knew it, too. It would only be a matter of time before Tancred or one of his men sought revenge.

That time came when Chesham was assigned to dig ditches outside the prison walls with about hundred other prisoners – including Tancred. There were more than thirty guards standing around watching the prisoners as they worked. The guards were armed with pistols and shotguns, and in the turret above the wall of the prison behind them were two more guards armed with rifles. The men in Pile Territorial Penitentiary were considered the worst of the worst in all of New Mexico, and the warden was taking no chances.

The prisoners had been roused an hour before dawn, when it was still cold out. The rising sun soon warmed them, and then the warmth turned into a blistering summer heat. The rags the prisoners wore as 'uniforms' were soaked through as they picked and shoveled the hard ground. Chesham had started at the end of the line, near the wall. He had noted Tancred's position about halfway up the line of laboring prisoners.

After two hours, the guards called a halt to the work and allowed the men to come out of the ditch to drink water from giant iron tubs set on tables. It hadn't passed Chesham's notice that Tancred was steadily moving closer and closer to him as they worked.

7

Chesham plunged the dipper into the lukewarm water and held it to his lips, drinking deeply. He noticed nervous glances from a few other prisoners, and saw a group of men – rapists and murderers all – clustered around Tancred. There was an atmosphere of expectation. He took another gulp of water and assessed his chances if Tancred decided to take him on, one on one.

Tancred was a huge man, standing about six-and-a-half feet tall. He had thick dark hair and a bushy beard, with broad shoulders and massive arms. He was going to fat now, but Chesham had no illusions about how strong the man was. He had seen Tancred beat down some of the biggest and strongest men in the Pile. He knew what he was capable of – and he knew how dirty Tancred fought, too.

After one last drink from the dipper, Chesham went back to work. He saw that Tancred was now even closer, with only about five men separating them. He feigned indifference as he dug, not wanting to put the big man on guard before the attack. He wanted his retaliation to come as a complete surprise to Butch Tancred.

Another hour passed, and then another. Still Tancred remained where was, making no move in Chesham's direction. Chesham began to wonder if he had misjudged the situation. He had, after all, been prepared for the worst ever since he had refused to obey Tancred's command.

The guards called the men up for another water break. Chesham turned to put down his shovel, and suddenly the five men between him and Tancred moved aside as one, making an opening for Tancred.

For such a physically colossal man, Tancred moved with startling swiftness. He closed the gap between him and Chesham in barely a second, raising his pick above his head. Chesham crouched and thrust the blade of his shovel just under Tancred's sternum. Tancred groaned, dropping his arms but maintaining a loose grip on his pick. His face was a deep crimson as he struggled to get a breath, and Chesham knew the time to strike was now. He also knew that he would have to kill Tancred, here and now, if he wanted a chance of surviving another day in the Pile. Despite the misery of his daily existence, Chesham certainly wanted to stay alive; and if he had to die, he was damn sure going to take Butch Tancred with him.

Chesham swung the shovel again, taking Tancred in the side of the head. But Tancred had been seized by blood lust and, although he swayed on his feet for a moment, he didn't go down. Instead he lunged forward, still struggling to breathe, and took another swing at Chesham's skull with his pick. Chesham ducked and felt the air move as the blade of the pick passed a mere few inches over the top of his head. When it had passed, he leapt upward, smashing the top of his head into Tancred's chin. Tancred

9

shrieked and dropped his pick, blood pouring from between his dark yellow teeth. His eyes were glassy with pain as he put his hand to his mouth and spit almost half of his tongue into his palm. He had bitten clean through it.

Tancred stumbled backward a few steps, struggling to yell something at Chesham. All that came out were garbled sounds. Then he looked down at the pick on the ground and stepped toward it, his face twisted with murderous rage. His fingers had almost gripped the handle when Chesham stooped and picked it up first. He grasped it solidly and, before his opponent had time to react, slammed it into the side of Tancred's head, the blade sinking up to the handle. Tancred fell over on his side, the pick lodged in his cranium. Blood still pumped from his mouth for a few seconds as he stared vacantly into the blazing sun, and then his heart stopped and he stared into oblivion.

Exhausted, Chesham sat down on the edge of the ditch. He realized then that a crowd had gathered to watch the festivities, brief though they were. The expressions on the men's faces were of disbelief and grudging respect. Chesham had killed the most dangerous and feared man in the Pile. As far as he was concerned, he had done what he had to do to stay alive. He knew he was lucky that Tancred hadn't actually gotten his hands on him, because the outcome would almost certainly have been much different.

He looked up and saw that the guards in the watchtower had witnessed the entire thing. One of them smiled at Chesham and doffed his hat. Chesham wiped sweat away from his eyes and looked down at Tancred's body. A feeling of enormous relief flowed through him.

The sound of a guard yelling caused him to look to his right. The crowd parted and three guards approached on the edge of the ditch, looking at the bloody corpse with the pick protruding from its head. One of the guards looked at Chesham.

'You did this?' he asked incredulously.

Chesham nodded. 'Afraid so,' he said evenly. 'It was him or me.'

The guard rubbed a hand across his jaw, assessing the situation.

'I'll be damned,' he said. 'Never thought I'd see the day someone got the better of Butch Tancred.' He squinted as he looked at the body. 'And by God, you sure got the better of him.'

'Like I said,' Chesham replied. 'It was him or me.'

The guard looked at Chesham curiously for a moment, then turned to the other guards. 'All right, fellers. Take him in. The warden's going to want to see him.'

Chesham rose and the two guards grabbed him roughly and began to shove him toward the main gate of the prison. As he was led away, he heard the guards ordering the men back to work. He also

11

heard someone ask, 'Who's going to pull that thing out of his head?' There were no volunteers.

Although he didn't mourn the passing of Butch Tancred, the warden had absolutely no tolerance for violence among the prisoners. In fact, the issue had been one of the determining factors in his appointment as warden to begin with. The governor had said he wanted a 'hard man' to tame the prisoners of Pile Territorial Penitentiary. The warden had promised to be that man.

He decided to make an example of Hank Chesham. He had no other choice.

The warden sentenced Chesham to six months in solitary, in the far room of Cell Block C. Solitary confinement meant more than just isolation from the rest of the prison population. It meant reduced rations – a chunk of moldy bread and one cup of water per day – in a cell that was exposed to the sun throughout the daytime hours, during the height of the New Mexican summer. It would almost surely constitute a death sentence.

After four weeks, Chesham was near death. His weight had dropped to the point where his ribs and hip bones protruded. His skin was parched from dehydration. He had trouble seeing, was constantly lightheaded, and walked in a shuffle. Sometimes he even hallucinated.

He certainly thought he was hallucinating the day

he heard the hinges of his cell door creak and opened his eyes to see the warden standing in the doorway, looking down at him with a strangely neutral expression, containing neither contempt nor compassion. Chesham blinked a few times before he recognized the man, but he still wasn't sure if what he was seeing was real or not.

'Chesham,' the warden said. 'Get up.'

The prisoner tried to obey, but his weakness undermined him. Only on his third try was he able to reach his feet and stay on them. He leaned against the wall for support as his head spun.

'Afternoon, warden,' he said weakly. 'What's the occasion?'

'You're free, Chesham.'

Now I know I'm seeing things, thought Chesham. Hearing things, too.

'I'm . . . free?'

'You heard me. You've been ordered released by Judge Owens. I'll have one of the guards bring your clothes. Then you're free to go. I want you off the grounds of this prison within the hour. Understood?'

Chesham stared at the warden's face for several seconds, gradually realizing that his head wasn't playing games with him. This was really happening.

'Understood, sir.'

The warden turned to the nearest guard. 'Get him his clothes, and then bring him to my office.' He glanced back at Chesham. 'The judge died last night

13

and this was his last action in office. He also left you a thousand dollars in his will. I'll give it to you when you're ready to leave.'

With those words, the warden turned on his heel and walked down the corridor. The guards followed behind him.

They left the cell door open.

CHAPTER ONE

Hank Chesham pulled reins and patted his sorrel's mane. The sky was darkening, and Chesham knew that soon a heavy rain would be pouring down on him. He sighed and removed his slicker from one of his saddle-bags. Before putting it on, he fingered the makings from his pocket and built a cigarette.

'It's going to be a wet night, girl,' he muttered to the horse.

He thumb-snapped a lucifer and held it to his smoke, inhaling deeply. He had halted on the ridge of a small, densely forested Oregon valley. Giant fir trees towered imperiously above and below him, suffused by a thick mist. There was a strange stirring in his chest as his keen gray eyes took in the scenery.

He was, at last, home.

He almost couldn't believe it. For five years, he had rotted in a New Mexico prison, arrested, tried, and convicted for a crime he didn't commit. There were many days when he thought he would die – indeed, when death would have come as a welcome reprieve. But Hank Chesham was alive, and he was home.

By the time he finished his cigarette, it had already started to rain. He flicked the small remnant of his smoke on to the ground, and the ember hissed as the rain drops extinguished it. Chesham donned his slicker and pulled the brim of his dun Stetson down a little further on his head. He heeled his mount through the trees and descended into the valley.

The rain increased steadily as he made his way down to the bottom. He decided to call it a day and moved to the edge of a clearing to make camp. Exhaustion had Chesham in its grip and all he wanted was some food and sleep.

He moved beneath a canopy of trees and dismounted. Very little rain made its way through here. Picketing his horse, he removed the saddle and rubbed the animal down with a blanket. He put some oats in a bag and placed it over the sorrel's head. The wetness precluded a fire, so Chesham had no choice but to have a cold camp, although he would dearly have liked to warm his frigid limbs. He took down his bedroll and rolled into his blankets as dusk spread across the sky, barely discernible behind the now-black clouds. He ate some hard tack and some jerky, then laid his head against his saddle and fell into a deep slumber.

Chesham slept for nearly four hours. When he awoke, it was a little after midnight. The rain had stopped, although water dripped off the branches of the trees. He was less cold than he had been earlier. He could see his horse standing in the shadows nearby. His tired mind turned back to the unlikely events that had led to his release from prison and subsequent return to Oregon.

He had been arrested five years before, in an alley outside a saloon in Santa Fe. He had made the long journey south to settle the estate of his brother. Art Chesham had moved to New Mexico more than a decade ago, and during those years in the desert he had established himself a very successful cattle agent. His sudden death had terminated his lucrative career. Art had been thrown from a horse and suffered a major head injury. He lingered unconscious for a few days before dying. The telegram reached Hank Chesham some days later, and as his brother's only surviving relative he had immediately headed out to fulfill his familial duty.

Everything had gone smoothly. Art had left his brother his entire estate, totaling more than seven thousand dollars. Chesham transferred the funds to his bank account in Oregon and, after tying up a few other loose ends, decided to have a couple beers at a saloon located four blocks from his hotel. He was due to leave for Oregon the next morning.

He had finished his drinks and was looking

forward to a restful night's sleep. He exited the saloon and passed through a narrow walkway that led to an alley. That was when the two men emerged from the darkness and stood before him.

'Hank Chesham?' one of the men asked.

Chesham halted. 'Yes,' he said. 'Do I know you?'

The man smiled and pulled back his heavy trench coat, revealing the star on his chest. It glinted in the moonlight.

'I'm the town marshal,' he said. He was a large man with a bulging belly. His dark eyes sparkled malevolently. 'Name's Jack Borg.'

Something about the man's tone was mildly alarming to Chesham.

'How can I help you, Marshal?' he asked.

Borg sneered. 'You can help me by taking that pistol out of your holster,' he said. 'You're under arrest.'

A cold tingle snaked down Chesham's spine. 'What the hell are you talking about?' he asked. 'Under arrest for what?'

The other figure had lingered in the shadows, but now he stepped up beside Borg. He was also a large man, with a tawny mustache and bushy sideburns. His lips were pulled back from his teeth in a snarl. Chesham knew the man would like nothing more than to have an excuse to start a fight.

'You don't ask the questions here, feller,' said the second man.

Chesham spotted a tin star on this man's chest, too. A tarnished star. He must be a deputy marshal.

'I ask questions when someone tells me I'm under arrest,' Chesham said coldly. 'Especially when I ain't broken any laws.'

'Maybe you got a hearing problem,' Borg said. He turned to his deputy, a sarcastic expression covering his face. 'That must be it, Phil. He didn't hear me tell him to hand over that pistol.'

'What the hell is this all about?' Chesham demanded.

His eyes flicked around the alley and he realized there was no escape route. Whatever was happening here, Chesham didn't trust the two lawmen who were trying to take him into custody. Not one bit.

'You'll hear all about it when you surrender peaceably,' said Borg.

Both men took another step, closing the already small distance between themselves and Chesham.

'We got ourselves a real smart-mouthed polecat here, Marshal,' said the man called Phil.

Chesham looked toward Borg, and as he did so, Phil made his move. He leaned forward, his arm darting out toward Chesham's holster. Chesham's fist shot forward, clipping Phil on the jaw. The deputy's head snapped sideways, and he folded at the waist and collapsed on to the ground in an untidy heap.

Chesham raised his head toward Jack Borg, and the last thing he saw was the butt of a shotgun swooping downward toward his skull. Then darkness engulfed him and he, too, fell to the ground.

It was the beginning of a nightmare that wouldn't end for five long, bitter years.

On the cold ground beneath the canopy of branches, Chesham adjusted the saddle behind his head and forced himself to stop thinking about the events from five years before. He had thought about them so many times, and he knew it was futile to try to make sense of them. What mattered now is that he had, miraculously, been released from jail. He was back home, and from now on his mind would focus on the future – the future that he had long thought would never come.

Eventually he fell asleep again, not awakening until dawn began to supplant the darkness in the sky. He rose, shivering in the November morning air, and broke camp. He saddled his horse, ate a little more jerky, and rode out, heading north.

After so many weeks on the trail, the knowledge that he would be back at his ranch in about eight hours was almost exhilarating. He was avoiding the main trails, riding through the foot hills of the southern Willamette Valley. His ranch, the Rimrock, was located about twenty miles east of Springfield. He wanted to get there without attracting any undue attention.

Chesham's wife, Phoebe, hadn't written to him

while he was in prison. He sent her several letters during the first year of his imprisonment. He didn't receive even a single reply to the letters he sent. After a time, he had stopped writing.

Was she dead? Had she abandoned him? Was she still even at the Rimrock? He had asked himself the same questions a million times, never thinking the day would come when he could find answers for himself. But today was that day.

Phoebe, he knew, couldn't run the ranch by herself. She hadn't been raised on a ranch, and only her love for Hank Chesham had led her to live on one. The Rimrock had only been in operation for a year when he left for New Mexico. His desire to see what it looked like now, and to find Phoebe, was intense.

It was mid-afternoon when he climbed the high incline and reached the summit of the small mountain that marked the eastern edge of the Rimrock ranch. The front of the mountain was a sheer rock wall, a hundred feet high. Trees covered the top of the mountain, and Chesham alighted and tied his mare to one of them.

He opened a saddle-bag and removed a pair of field glasses from them. He made his way through the trees to the top of the rock wall. There, he knelt and raised the glasses to his eyes. As he looked down on to the Rimrock, he inhaled sharply.

It had been a flourishing operation when

21

Chesham had left, but now, as his glasses moved from the main house to the stables to the bunkhouses to the corrals, he saw that it had grown into one of the major ranching outfits in this area of Oregon. Chesham knew ranching, and there was no mistaking what the Rimrock had become.

The main house had been considerably expanded. It now had a second story, and a large awninged veranda had been built around its entire perimeter. He could see an elderly woman dressed in a servant's uniform, hanging laundry on a line behind the house. He didn't recognize her.

There were men coming out of the bunkhouse, moving toward the cook shack for their afternoon meal. More than a dozen men, in fact. The ranch had to be bringing in significant amounts of money to support that many ranch hands. He watched them stride into the cook shack. Smoke billowed into the air from its chimney.

Chesham scanned the other buildings on the property again, and then his glance swept over the rest of the valley that constituted the ranch. Thousands of cattle grazed across the verdant pastures. To his left, near the line of foothills that bordered the property, large, sturdy fences enclosed several acres of land where at least a hundred horses milled.

Chesham lowered his field glasses, his face grim. He didn't know what to make of the scene below. It was as if his grandest ambitions for the ranch had been achieved – all while he sat locked in a dirty prison cell, year after year. He didn't know what he had expected to find when he rode back to the Rimrock, but it certainly wasn't this.

Movement at the far end of the valley pulled Chesham away from his thoughts. He raised the field glasses and fixed his gaze there. His mouth tightened as his mind registered what he was seeing. It was a woman, riding a large, beautiful chestnut horse. She passed quickly through the gates of the ranch and moved toward the main house. She wore a blue checked shirt and riding pants, the bottoms of which were covered by dark leather boots. Her hat lay down her back, hanging by the strap around her neck. Chesham focused on her features: the pale white skin, the firm but feminine jaw, the lustrous blonde hair that she had tied in a pony tail.

There was no mistaking who this woman was. It was Phoebe Chesham, and she was as beautiful as she had ever been.

Chesham watched her ride, impressed by the skill and confidence with which she handled the massive animal beneath her. This was an entirely new Phoebe, who had never had much assurance with horses. In her husband's absence, she had clearly improved her horsemanship – to put it mildly.

Strange emotions stirred within Hank Chesham as he watched her approach the main house – longing, sadness, and a deep feeling of love, the love he had felt for her since the day they first met, nearly ten years before. Why hadn't she written him? It was clear that she had moved on with her life, although her motivations were a mystery. He had many questions he wanted to ask her.

Chesham watched her slow the horse as she came into the yard in front of the house. She rode around the side and made her way to the back yard. The door to the stable opened and a man came out and took her reins as she alighted. He turned and led the horse toward the stable.

Phoebe pulled off her hat and shook her hair out. Then she turned suddenly as a man exited the back door of the house and stood on the steps of the veranda. She smiled and ran toward him, and he embraced her. They kissed and then stood together talking, the man's arms still encircling her.

Chesham's pulse roared in his ears as he took in the scene. And then he recognized the man, and a cold, deadly rage grew within him. He pushed himself to his feet and walked back from the cliff into the trees.

CHAPTER TWO

It took Chesham nearly forty-five minutes to descend the back of the mountain and ride around to the front gate of the Rimrock. He noted that the fences that had been built in his absence were of very high quality. He rode out of the woods on to the road and heeled his horse toward the gate. The two large poles that bordered the entrance to the property were joined above by a massive wrought-iron sign that said RIMROCK. He rode through the gate and headed for the main house at a steady but unhurried pace.

In the fields on either side of the road were at least ten of the ranch hands. Chesham could feel their eyes on him as he rode past. He turned and returned their stares. By God, this was his land. He wasn't some interloper.

Adrenaline was coursing through his veins, and he struggled to control his emotions. The adrenaline wasn't a sign of nervousness or uncertainty, but rather profound shock at what he had witnessed when Phoebe rode up to the house. He didn't want to say or do anything rash, but he was going to ask some hard questions.

Chesham had hoped to have a private conversation with Phoebe, but that was out of the question now.

He pulled leather and dismounted near the front of the house. The large front door opened and Phoebe walked out on to the veranda. She looked at Chesham as if she didn't recognize him, and then he realized she probably didn't recognize him. He was much thinner than he had been five years before, and the weeks on the trail had left him looking dirty and haggard. His beard was thick and hung halfway down to his chest.

'Hello, Phoebe,' he said evenly. 'Don't you recognize your own husband?'

Her face flushed and her eyes widened in disbelief. She drew a sharp breath and her hand reached up and touched her throat.

'My God,' she rasped. 'Hank?'

A sour grin quirked the corner's of Chesham's mouth. 'The one and only,' he said.

Phoebe made no move to approach him. 'But . . . how?' she asked.

'It's a long story,' he said. 'I'm starting to think you're not happy to see me.'

She blinked a few times, trying to assess the situation. 'Hank, I—'

Her words were silenced by the opening of the

26

front door behind her. She turned and looked as the man Chesham had seen embracing her earlier walked confidently up to her and encircled her with a comforting arm. He squinted as he cast an appraising glance at Hank Chesham.

'Good Lord,' the man said. 'It's Hank Chesham.'

Chesham nodded. 'Ted Flynn,' he replied. 'Never thought I'd see you again. Definitely never thought I'd see you putting your hands on my wife like that, either.'

Flynn's blunt features hardened at Chesham's words. 'Phoebe isn't your wife anymore, my friend,' he said. 'Phoebe is my wife now.'

Chesham removed his Stetson and patted it gently against the side of his leg.

'That right?' he asked.

'Yes, that's right,' Flynn retorted. He squeezed Phoebe a little closer to him. 'Ain't it, honey?'

Phoebe seemed to wither under Chesham's intent stare. Finally, she spoke.

'Yes, it is.'

Chesham's eyes slitted. 'Well, isn't this an interesting turn of events,' he said, his tone clipped. 'You realize this is still my land, don't you, Ted?'

Flynn smirked. 'I'm afraid you're wrong about that, too, Hank,' he said. 'I bought this ranch from the bank a year after you went to prison. It's in my name – every square foot of it.'

Chesham dropped his horse's reins and stepped forward, his right hand moving down toward the

Navy revolver on his hip. 'You better move away from him, Phoebe,' he said.

Ted Flynn's face was impassive, except for a strange twitch in his cheek, just under his left eye. 'Don't be a fool, Hank,' he said. 'You best just get back on that horse and ride out. There ain't nothing here for you anymore.'

'You going to move, Phoebe? I wouldn't want you to get hurt while I'm killing Ted.'

That got the reaction Chesham was looking for. The twitch in Flynn's cheek increased, and there was an unmistakable hint of fear in his eyes as he removed his arm from Phoebe's shoulders and pushed her back toward the front door.

'Go on, honey,' he said.

Phoebe took one last look at Chesham, then moved toward the door and went inside the house.

'I figured you'd use her as a shield, Ted,' Chesham said. 'I guess you're a little tougher than I thought.'

Flynn made no move toward his pistol. Instead, he stood in place, eyeing Chesham warily.

'Before you get ahead of yourself, Hank, you should know that we were told you'd never get out of prison,' he said. 'The Rimrock was going to hell, real quick. Phoebe didn't know what to do. I gave you more than three thousand dollars to build this place, and I couldn't afford to lose that. It ain't like we planned all this.'

'You can have Phoebe,' Chesham said. 'I don't

know what happened between you two, but I suspect the worst. As far as I'm concerned, you deserve each other. But if you think you can take my ranch, you're sorely mistaken.'

'This is my ranch now, Hank. The sooner you get that in your head, the better.'

'I think it's time we let our guns do the talking, you four-flushing sack of shit.'

Flynn grimaced and his hand lunged downward to his gun. He cleared leather and then froze in place, his pistol only raised halfway. Hank Chesham's pistol was pointed directly at his chest, the hammer already pulled back. The pistol in Flynn's hand shook.

'You never were fast on the draw, Ted,' Chesham observed, his hands perfectly steady. 'You made a mighty big mistake when you tried to take my land. Now you're going to give back what's rightfully mine.'

'Wh-what do you mean?' Flynn asked.

'We're going to go inside the house – my house – and you're going to sign over the Rimrock to me. Then I'm going to give you and Phoebe one day to clear out. We clear?'

Flynn's incredulity was nearly as strong as his fear. 'You're downright loco, pard,' he said.

'From where I'm standing, it looks like I hold all the cards, Teddie boy. Now drop that pistol on the porch and turn around.'

Flynn hesitated momentarily, considering his options. He had known Hank Chesham for over a decade, and he knew he was a strong-willed individual. The flinty look on Chesham's face told Flynn that the man meant what he said. In that moment, he knew that Chesham wouldn't hesitate to kill him where he stood. Flynn opened his fingers and allowed his pistol to fall on to the plank floor of the veranda. Then he slowly turned around, facing toward the door. He heard Chesham's boots crunch in the gravel as he walked to the steps. Chesham stopped on the veranda and picked up Flynn's gun, which he tossed into the bushes a few feet away. Then he pressed his pistol hard into Flynn's back and shoved him toward the door.

'Move your ass,' he said.

Flynn complied, opening first the screen door and then the huge oak door that lead into the foyer. Chesham followed him in, then hooked the heel of his boot on the door and pushed it closed behind them. They moved down the hallway to the office. Phoebe sat in a chair near the window, her eyes wide with alarm and her hands covering her mouth. She lowered her hands when she saw Chesham and his gun.

'What are you going to do, Hank?' she asked.

'Just settle back and see,' said Chesham. There was a desk on the other side of the room. Chesham pushed Flynn toward it. 'Have a seat.'

Flynn pulled out the chair and sat down. He looked at Phoebe, his face ashen.

'Get out some paper and write down what I say,' Chesham commanded. 'And if you have a gun in the desk and are thinking about trying anything cute, just remember I'll blast you out of that chair.'

Flynn's jaw was clenched as he glared at Chesham. He opened a drawer and removed a sheet of paper, then plucked his pen from its stand on the blotter and dipped it in the inkwell.

'Write the following,' Chesham said. 'This document is to certify that Henry Chesham is the rightful owner of the Rimrock Ranch, and that we conspired to steal it from him while he was imprisoned. We hereby cede all ownership of the Rimrock to Mr. Chesham and agree to vacate the property within twenty-four hours.'

Flynn's hand shook as he wrote, the tip of the pen making rapid scratching sounds on the paper. Flynn didn't look up when he finished writing. It was as if he couldn't bear to look at Hank Chesham.

'Now sign it,' Chesham said. When Flynn complied, Chesham turned to Phoebe. 'You sign it, too.'

Phoebe rose and crossed to the desk. She took the pen and wrote 'Phoebe Flynn' in her characteristically neat handwriting.

Chesham felt a momentary pang when he saw what she had written. He took the pen from her and dated the document, which he folded and placed in the inside pocket of his sheepskin coat. He looked from Ted Flynn's face to Phoebe's, his mouth a grim line of determination.

'I'm going into town to present this to the court. I

think you both know me well enough to understand that I ain't playing around here. The Rimrock is mine, and it always was. If you're not off the land by this time tomorrow, I'll remove you both myself. You can make this easy or hard. Makes no difference to me.'

Still holding his gun before him, Chesham backed toward the parlor door and stepped into the hallway. He strode quickly out of the house and mounted his horse, which he neck-reined toward the gate. He touched spurs and his horse burst into a gallop. The ranch hands watched him ride by, not sure what to make of the stranger. Chesham was glad that none of them had heard the discussion in the yard, or seen him pull his gun on Ted Flynn. They had been too far out in the pastures.

He passed through the gate and slowed the horse. He looked back toward the house and spotted Flynn standing on the porch, watching him. Chesham gave him a wave and then turned left on the road to Eugene.

After a mile or two, Hank Chesham turned off the main road and kneed his mount through a thicket of trees. He dismounted and tied the reins to a sapling. He was completely obscured from the road, and from his position he could see for nearly a half-mile back in the direction from which he had come. He kept an eye on his back trail for five minutes, watching to see if Flynn or any of his men had decided to pursue him. Satisfied that no one was following, he leaned against a tree and felt for the makings. He constructed a cigarette and tried to organize his thoughts.

Ted Flynn was in the forefront of his mind. Chesham had long since come to the conclusion that Phoebe had probably betrayed him; the only other possibility he had considered during his years of imprisonment was that she might be dead. But he had never really believed that. He had figured that the reason she hadn't written and never made any attempt to help him was because she had cut him off.

But Ted Flynn? The idea that she had betrayed him for Flynn boggled his mind. Chesham had known Flynn for more years than he had known Phoebe. Flynn was a mid-level rancher and horse trader with whom Chesham had done business on many occasions over the years. When Chesham took the plunge and bought the Rimrock, Flynn had invested in the undertaking and been very encouraging. Although they had never been close friends, their interactions had always been positive and mutually beneficial.

But now. . . . Ted Flynn had stolen Hank Chesham's wife and his ranch. He had betrayed Chesham as profoundly as any man could. And Phoebe had been a willing accomplice. Chesham recalled their embrace in the yard behind the house. It was abundantly clear that Phoebe was in love with

Flynn; this was no marriage of convenience, although greed must have been a factor in bringing them together.

Had they planned all this before he even left for New Mexico? Nothing would surprise Chesham now.

He rubbed out his cigarette on the bark of a tree and removed the sheet of paper from his pocket. He unfolded it and read it again. He had no idea if it would hold water with the judge in Eugene; in fact, he doubted it would. But it had allowed him to humiliate Flynn and to shame Phoebe. Short of killing them, it was the most potent statement he could make in response to their betrayal.

He pulled out his silver pocket watch and opened it. The spidery hands told him it was a few minutes after four o'clock. He wouldn't make it to Eugene before the courthouse closed. He would have to see the judge in the morning. He replaced the watch and untied his sorrel.

Chesham knew what he had to do this evening. There was one person he needed to see – his former sister-in-law, Mandy. Phoebe's sister. She had always been a good friend to him, and if anyone could answer his questions, Mandy could.

He untied his horse and climbed into the saddle. A few seconds later he was back on the road to Eugene.

CHAPTER THREE

It was six o'clock when Hank Chesham rode into Eugene. Dusk was settling in behind a bank of dark clouds. The town had grown considerably in the five years since Chesham had last seen it.

Chesham rode up a busy street on the south side of town, pulling leather in front of a small café. The sign in the window said 'closed'. He dismounted and threw his reins over the hitching post. When he climbed the steps to the boardwalk and looked through the window, he saw her clearing the tables. It was her, all right – Mandy Smith, the younger sister of his wife. Or, rather, Ted Flynn's wife.

He tapped on the window and she looked toward him. It was obvious she didn't recognize him as she approached the front of the café. She unlocked the door and opened it a few inches.

'I'm sorry, sir,' she said, 'but we're closed now.'

'Hello, Mandy,' said Chesham. She squinted, and

then recognition came to her. 'It's me – Hank.'

A grin spread across her face and she opened the door.

'Hank!' She embraced him, still looking up into his face as if she couldn't believe it was him. 'I thought I'd never see you again.'

'So did I,' he said drily, as he stepped into the café.

'When did you get into town?' she asked.

'A couple of hours ago. I stopped in at the Rimrock before I came to see you.'

The smile left her face. 'Oh. I suppose that must have been something of a shock.'

He nodded. 'You could say that.'

She closed the door and locked it again, not sure what to say. 'I'm sure you've got a lot of questions about what happened between Phoebe and Ted.'

'That I do.'

'Well, I'll tell you everything I know. Are you hungry?'

Chesham realized he hadn't eaten since early that morning. 'I'm definitely hungry.'

She smiled. 'Good. Come on back to the kitchen and I'll feed you.'

He followed her past the tables through a doorway into the kitchen. There was a small table across from the oven, and Chesham pulled out a chair and sat down. Mandy pulled the lid of a pot and looked inside.

'We got a lot of elk stew left over. Would that suit you?'

'Sounds good,' he said.

She ladled stew into a large tin bowl and handed it to him, along with a spoon. She brought over a basket with some rolls in it and he accepted them gratefully. He ate ravenously, happy to have something to think about other than Ted, Phoebe, and the Rimrock.

Mandy sat down across the table from Chesham and watched him eat. He could feel her eyes studying him.

'It sure is good to see you, Hank,' she said. 'From what I'd been told, you were never going to get out of jail.'

Chesham broke a roll open and dipped it in the stew. He took a bite and chewed thoughtfully.

'It's pretty strange how it happened,' he said. 'The judge who tried and sentenced me ordered that I be released. He was on his death bed.'

Mandy frowned. 'What's the story there?'

He shrugged. 'I don't know. He was dead when I was released. He left me a thousand dollars, too. Told people he'd done a terrible thing in locking me up.' He took another bite of stew. 'I used his money to buy my horse and come home.' He looked up. 'It's too bad he was dead, because I would have liked to talk to him about his change of heart.'

'Strange,' said Mandy. 'What were you locked up for to begin with?'

'I got jumped in an alley by a two-bit crooked

37

marshal and his deputy,' he explained. 'They claimed I held up a stage outside Santa Fe. They even had a witness who said he recognized my horse. The judge sentenced me to twenty years. I didn't know anyone in New Mexico, so there was no one to help me.'

'I'm sorry, Hank. It's just terrible that that happened to you.'

'Thanks, Mandy. If there's such a thing as hell on earth, it's the prison in Santa Fe.'

'What was it like?'

Chesham finished his meal and started making a cigarette. 'Burning hot in the day and freezing cold at night. The only thing they feed you is slop. Hell, I wouldn't feed that to pigs. Sometimes they'd work us for twenty hours straight, in the sun with no shade. Other times they'd leave us in our cells for weeks at a time.' He twisted the end of the cigarette and poked it between his lips. It bobbed up and down as he spoke. 'Some real nasty characters there, too. You really have to watch your back. Some of the guards were just as bad as the rapists and murderers.'

'How did you survive it?'

Chesham struck a match and pulled smoke into his lungs. 'I don't know. I really don't. There were a lot of days when I would rather have been dead than in that jail. Especially after I realized Phoebe had abandoned me.'

'Yes,' said Mandy in a soft voice. 'That must have

made it much harder to bear.'

Chesham removed the cigarette from his mouth and examined it.

'What's the story, Mandy?' he asked. 'I came close to blasting Ted Flynn to hell this afternoon. I had no idea about . . . him and Phoebe.' His face was set in harsh lines as he spoke. 'When did it start?'

Mandy exhaled slowly. 'I only became aware of it after you'd left for New Mexico. Everyone in town was talking about how you'd been arrested and sent to prison. Next thing I know, Ted Flynn starts spending a lot of time out at the Rimrock. I didn't know what to make of it. He said he was helping Phoebe run the place, and that he was a part owner.'

'That lying bastard,' Chesham said. 'He helped me buy it, but he was never a part owner. We made an agreement that I'd pay him back with interest within three years.'

'I figured he was lying,' Mandy affirmed. 'Then one day I hear that Phoebe and Ted have gone up to Salem and gotten married. She told me with you in prison for at least the next twenty years, she had no other choice but to get the marriage annulled. She said that her relationship with Ted started out purely as a business arrangement after you left, but that she fell in love with him. That's all I know.'

'Seems he's done real well for himself.'

'He owns a lot of property over in Eugene and Springfield now. The general store and the livery. He owns a boarding house, too. He has an office at the back there.'

Chesham's eyes were distant as stared at a spot on the wall. 'I guess I never really knew Phoebe after all. I thought I did, but the woman I knew wouldn't ever have done something like this. I'm sure Flynn spearheaded the whole thing, but Phoebe went along with it, all the way.' He met her gaze. 'That means she's going to pay for it, right along with Ted.'

Mandy's face colored. 'What do you mean, Hank?'

'Ted can have Phoebe,' Chesham said thinly. 'But the Rimrock is mine. I'll kill him before I let him take it from me.'

'How are you going to get it back from him? I think he went through all the right legal steps to buy it.'

'That may be. But he'll either give up the ranch to me, or I'll make him wish I'd died in that jail.' He smirked. 'Hell, he probably already wishes that.' He reached into his coat pocket and removed the paper he had forced Flynn and Phoebe to sign. 'I have this, too. Don't know if it'll hold up in court, though.'

He passed the paper over the table to Mandy, who read it eagerly.

'They both signed it,' she said. 'How'd you get them to do that?'

'I had a little help from Mr. Colt,' he said.

'They'll probably claim you forced them sign it.'

'I'm sure they will.'

'So what then?'

'That remains to be seen,' Chesham said, rolling another cigarette. 'I'll tell you this, though – that ranch will never be Ted Flynn's. Come hell or high water, his days at the Rimrock are numbered. And he knows I'm not just flapping my gums.'

Mandy Smith's face was solemn as she listened to Chesham speak. She knew that he wasn't a malicious man, and that he had endured five terrible years only to return home and find that everything he cared about had been taken away from him, by people he trusted. As she took in his words, she realized that he could be provoked to violence over the Rimrock. She had no doubt that, if it came down to it, he would kill Ted Flynn rather than back down.

'I wish there was something I could do to help you, Hank,' she said. 'You've been through so much.'

Chesham made a dismissive gesture. 'I appreciate that, Mandy. I don't want to have you drawn into this mess. I can handle it. Plus, you just gave me the best meal I've had in five years. So you've already helped more than you know.'

She smiled. 'I'm happy to feed you any time, Hank Chesham.'

'Be careful – I might take you up on that.'

They both laughed, and then there was a moment of awkward silence. Chesham realized that he had always been attracted to Mandy, although he had been devoted to Phoebe and would never have done

41

anything inappropriate with her sister. Mandy, too, was an honorable person.

Chesham pushed back his chair and rose to his feet.

'Well, thanks again, Mandy. It's good to see you. You haven't changed a bit. And your cooking's as good as ever.'

Mandy blushed. 'You always were a flatterer, Hank. Let me walk you to the door.'

She put her arm through his and they made their way through the tables to the front door. He opened the door and turned to her.

'I'll be seeing you again, real soon, if you'll have me.'

'Of course,' she said. 'You're always welcome here.'

He patted her on the arm and walked out into the night.

Chesham untied his horse and stepped into the saddle. The bracing night air refreshed him. He wheeled the animal up the street, wondering if the livery that used to be on the next block was still there.

There were few people on the sidewalks. The sorrel's hoofs make squelching noises in the thick mud. Three men were smoking cigars and chatting in front of the saloon on the corner. Chesham rode past them and then crossed the street. The livery was still there.

He rode through the open doors and made his way past the stalls to the back, where the stableman kept a small room. He alighted just as a man stepped out of the office.

'Can I help you?' the man asked.

'I'd like a stall for my horse, and to have her fed and watered.'

'Not a problem. You want to pay now or when you come get her?'

Chesham scratched at his beard. 'I'll pay when I come by in the morning. Is the Livermore Hotel still open?'

The man reached out and took the sorrel's reins. 'Yep, it is.'

'What time will you be open?'

'Seven o'clock.'

'I'll be here at seven.'

Chesham removed his saddle-bags and slung them over his shoulder. He made his way back to the front of the stable and exited out on to the street. The Livermore Hotel was a few blocks up. It had begun to rain and Chesham pulled up the collar of his coat against the chill.

He had nearly made it to the next block when a figure emerged from the shadows in front of a darkened dry goods store. The man had a cigar in his teeth, and his eyes glinted in the moonlight as he looked directly at Chesham. It took a few seconds for Chesham to realize that he was one of the men who had been standing in front of the saloon a few minutes before.

The man nodded in greeting as Chesham approached. 'Evening,' he said.

Chesham was nearly abreast of the man. He smiled and nodded back. At the same time, he struck out of with his right fist, taking the stranger in the throat. The man gasped and he clutched his neck, unable to speak. Chesham hit him with a hard left hook and the man's knees buckled.

The two other men from outside the saloon suddenly emerged from the dark alley beside the dry goods store. One was carrying a polished hickory stick, and before Chesham could reach for his gun, the man swung the stick hard into the side of his head. The skin split above his left ear and blood began to pour freely. Chesham struggled to remain conscious as the two men grabbed him and dragged him into the alley.

Anger and fear surged within Chesham. He rammed the back of his head into the face of one of the attackers. The man cried out, releasing Chesham and falling back into the shadows.

The man with the stick drove it hard into Chesham's ribs, knocking the wind out of him. As he struggled for air, Chesham reached out and gripped the stick, trying to twist it out of the man's hands. He pushed his arms forward and slammed the side of the stick into the man's chest, knocking him off-balance. Still the man held on, and they both tumbled into the mud.

Chesham kneed him in the stomach and leaned forward, his face inches from the other man's. 'Who sent you – Ted Flynn?'

The man opened his mouth to say something, but before he spoke Chesham felt strong hands grab him and pull him away. Then another man appeared, and Chesham recognized him as the one he had left on the sidewalk a minute earlier. Fists pummeled him, and he was only able to return a few punches before they had him on the ground.

His vision became blurry, and then he saw a blinding white light before losing consciousness.

CHAPTER FOUR

Mandy Smith couldn't sleep. She lay in her bed, her eyes wide open, in the small room behind her café. The rain pattered steadily against the window, and a small stream of moonlight spilled through the curtains.

She was thinking of Hank Chesham. The shock of seeing him after all those years had agitated her to the point of insomnia. It was a reminder to her of how powerful her feelings for him still were. Those same feelings that she had struggled for years to suppress. Now she recognized the futility of it all. Chesham was free and he was home. And no longer was he bound to Phoebe.

Mandy knew that Chesham was a fundamentally different man than he had been before he left for New Mexico. The trauma of his incarceration and now the betrayal by his wife and his closest associate – she saw a new anger and grimness in him that had never been there before. He had always been a positive, optimistic man, and that had been one of his most attractive qualities. Now that was gone, although her attraction for him remained.

Her thoughts turned to Phoebe and Ted Flynn. Her relationship with her sister had largely soured since the latter married Flynn. Although he was always friendly to her, Flynn struck Mandy as totally amoral, interested only in his own advancement and desires. She had tried to give him the benefit of the doubt, but nagging suspicions remained.

She wondered what Chesham would do to take back the Rimrock, and how Flynn would retaliate. Whatever happened, she knew that someone would end up getting hurt, or even killed.

Something thumped loudly against the back door, and Mandy abruptly sat up. Her breathing was shallow as she listened, but the only sound now was the rain. After a minute she relaxed and lay back on her pillow. She closed her eyes and tried to fall asleep. For the first time since she had gone to bed, she began to drift off.

Then the sound came again, but louder this time. A hard thudding against the door, followed by several quieter thumps.

Her heart pounding against her ribcage, Mandy slipped out of her bed and opened the top drawer of her dresser. A small snub-nosed pistol lay there. She removed it from the drawer and pulled back the hammer as she crossed the room toward the window. She paused by the curtain, then pulled it back only a few millimeters and peered through into the alley behind the café.

She gasped when she spotted the dark shape of a man lying near the door. His head rolled to the side and the moonlight illuminated his bloodied face, and then there was no doubt.

It was Hank Chesham.

Mandy tossed the pistol on to the bed and reached for the door handle. She pulled the door open and knelt beside Chesham. His hair was matted with blood, his eyes swollen almost shut, and his lips were cut. He was almost unrecognizable. Only the slight movement of his chest told her that he was still alive.

'Hank!' she cried. 'Hank, can you hear me?'

Chesham groaned and tried to blink. 'Mandy,' he murmured.

She put her arms under his shoulders and dragged him in from the rain-swept alleyway. She closed the door and locked it.

'Hank – who did this to you?' He coughed and tried to sit up, but she held him in place. 'Don't move yet. I'll be right back.'

She was gone for several minutes before returning with a pan of warm water and several cloths. She wetted the cloths and used them to wipe the blood from Chesham's face and neck. She removed his shirt. There were large, vicious-looking bruises across his abdomen. She touched them gently and he groaned again.

'I think you have a couple broken ribs,' she said, shaking her head. 'My God, who could do this?'

'Flynn,' said Chesham. 'They were . . . his men.'

'Are you sure?' she asked.

'Flynn,' he repeated. 'It was Flynn.'

'Did they try to kill you?'

He nodded faintly. 'They left me for dead.'

She said no more, focusing on helping Chesham. She cleaned him up as best she could, then helped him into the bed. He was obviously in tremendous pain, and not altogether coherent. Soon he was unconscious, although she wasn't sure if he had simply fallen asleep or had passed out. She spread some blankets down on the floor and swiftly fell into a troubled sleep.

The next day, Mandy Smith didn't open her café. It was the first day she had kept it closed in years. She tended to Chesham, feeding him soup and changing his bandages. He wasn't able to eat much and still seemed slightly disoriented. She had a powerful urge to summon the doctor, but she wouldn't allow herself to take the chance of revealing Chesham's location. She was confident that, were they to learn that Chesham was alive and hiding in the back of her café, the men who had attacked him would come again to finish the job.

In the late afternoon, Mandy unlocked the front

door and went out on to the sidewalk. She locked the door behind her. Chesham was asleep, and during his moments of relative alertness, she had begged him not to try to leave. He had agreed, and she reckoned he wasn't in any condition to leave even if he were so inclined.

She looked around the street, which was still bustling with activity. She turned and walked up to the livery. She was relieved to see that the old hostler was alone, shoveling hay into a stall. When she approached him, he looked up and smiled.

'Howdy, Miss Smith,' he said. 'Don't see you in here very often.'

'Good afternoon, Elvin,' she said, reassured by his friendly greeting. 'I think a man left his horse here with you last night. He was a big man, with a beard.'

The old man nodded. 'Yeah, he left his horse. A real pretty sorrel. He was supposed to come get her this morning.'

'Well, he wasn't able to make it.' She removed her small coin purse from a pocket on her dress. 'How much would it cost for you to keep his horse here until he's able to fetch her?'

He scrubbed a hand across his bewhiskered jaw. 'How long you think that'll be?'

'Ten days,' she said after a moment. 'Maybe two weeks.'

'It's a dollar a day, ma'am.'

She opened the coin purse and counted out ten

silver dollars. She put them in the man's hands and he slipped them into a pocket in his grubby pants.

'I'll come and give you more if he's not here in ten days,' she said.

'That's just fine, ma'am. I'll take real good care of her. Like I said, she's a beaut.'

'Thank you so much, Elvin,' she said.

She turned and exited back out on to the street. She walked down to the dry goods store where Chesham told her he had been attacked. When she peered into the alley beside it, there were large imprints in the mud where the struggle had taken place. She also spotted some blood smeared on the wall of the store. She pivoted and began making her way back toward the café. The alley where Chesham had nearly been killed was rarely used, and the signs of violence there didn't appear to have attracted any attention.

She returned to the café and spent the rest of the day tending to Hank Chesham.

Mandy was only able to keep the café closed for one day. She couldn't afford any more time off than that.

The days passed slowly. The combination of trying to run the restaurant and still nurse Chesham back to health was frequently overwhelming. Somehow, though, she managed. She was a very determined woman, and much tougher than was evident from outward appearances.

After ten days, she returned to the livery and gave the hostler another ten dollars. Chesham's recovery was slower than she had expected it to be, his injuries even more grievous than she had originally thought.

But there was no question that he was getting better. After two weeks, he was able to stand and walk around. The swelling on his face was gone, although there were now permanent scars where his lips had been cut. The bruising diminished gradually on his abdomen; in the first days after he was attacked, he couldn't even breathe without intense pain.

When she went to the store to buy food and other necessities, there was no discussion of the attack on Hank Chesham. Indeed, there was no apparent knowledge that Chesham had even returned. He had nearly been murdered on his first night back in Eugene, before he was able to encounter any old friends apart from Mandy. It was a relief to her to know that no one had any suspicions about Chesham or his whereabouts.

Then one day, toward the end of the third week of Chesham's recuperation, Phoebe Flynn entered the café just before closing time.

There were only a few customers in the restaurant. Mandy was busy loading dirty dishes on a tray to take back into the kitchen. She froze when her eyes met Phoebe's, but she quickly recovered.

'Hello, Phoebe,' she said.

Phoebe smiled wanly, apparently uncomfortable

in her sister's presence.

'Hello, Mandy,' she said, with forced levity. 'How've things been?'

'Fine. Busy as always.'

'Yes, yes. You work so hard.'

'It's how Ma and Pa raised us,' said Mandy.

'It certainly is.'

Mandy put the tray of dishes down on one of the tables. 'What brings you here?' she asked.

Phoebe looked around the room, then pulled out a chair and sat down. 'Oh, I was in town and thought I'd stop by to see how my little sister is doing.'

There was an unmistakable nervousness about Phoebe Flynn. Her sister had no trouble discerning its cause.

'Is everything all right, Phoebe?'

Phoebe looked down at her hands. She was squeezing them together so tightly that her knuckles were white. She raised her head and looked at Mandy.

'Hank came back,' she said softly. 'He got out of jail and came back a few weeks ago. He came out to the ranch. I thought he was going to kill Ted.'

'Where is he now?' Mandy asked.

'I don't know. He made us sign a piece of paper that said we stole the ranch from him, and then he rode out. Nobody's seen or heard from him since.'

Mandy was silent for a moment. 'Well, it looks like he skipped town. Maybe he decided he didn't want the Rimrock after all.'

Phoebe shook her head. 'I don't know. He loves that ranch. I can't see him giving up on getting it back.'

'Maybe he couldn't bear the thought of you being with Ted.'

'I know that hurt him,' said Phoebe. 'I can't do anything about that now. But. . . .' Her words faded, and again she squeezed her hands tightly.

'What is it, Phoebe?'

'I think Ted might have. . . .' She stopped speaking, as if she couldn't bring herself to say the words.

'Ted might have what?'

Phoebe's lips trembled as she spoke. 'He might have . . . done something to Hank.'

'Like what?' asked Mandy cautiously.

'He might have had him killed.'

'Would Ted do something like that?'

'I don't know,' said Phoebe. 'He's a very determined man, and if he decided Hank was a threat, he could be capable of anything.'

'How did you feel when you saw Hank?'

'It's hard to say. I was shocked more than anything. I never wanted to hurt him.' Phoebe sighed. 'What's done is done. I'm Ted's wife now. There's no going back. But I wouldn't ever have wanted Ted to do something to Hank.'

Mandy knew her sister was troubled by Chesham's return and subsequent disappearance. There were dark circles under Phoebe's eyes, and her skin was paler than Mandy had ever seen it. She also appeared to have lost weight. However, Mandy had a hard time mustering any sympathy for Phoebe. Hank had been through a terrible ordeal in New Mexico, and returned to Oregon to find that everything he held dear had been taken from him. And then the man responsible had tried to have him killed. Phoebe had played a very large role in the series of catastrophes that had befallen Hank Chesham – an honorable man who had always been devoted to her.

There was little Mandy could think to say to comfort Phoebe. She had made her own decisions, and now she would have to face the consequences. Mandy couldn't help but think that, when Chesham was fully recovered, there would be a lot more tribulation coming Phoebe's way.

Mandy rose, suddenly unable to continue her discussion with Phoebe.

'I'm sorry, but I have to close for the night and clean this place up,' she said.

Phoebe stood up. 'All right,' she said. 'Thanks for listening, anyway. We really should get together more often.'

Mandy arched an eyebrow. 'You say that every time we see each other.'

'I know, I know. But I mean it.'

Phoebe impulsively stepped forward and hugged her sister, something she had rarely done since they were children. Then she turned and walked hurriedly toward the door. She looked back at Mandy one last time before exiting out on to the street.

After closing up the café, Mandy opened the door to her bedroom. She found Chesham sitting in the chair near the back door, smoking a cigarette. His face was tight as he turned his head to look at her.

'Phoebe was here,' he said.

'How did you know?'

'I heard her voice. I would know it anywhere.'

She walked to a chair beside the bed and sat down. 'How do you feel about it?'

'The only thing I feel now is . . . anger.' He rested his head against the back of the chair and exhaled smoke toward the ceiling. 'I feel nothing for Phoebe.'

'I can't say I blame you,' said Mandy.

Chesham leaned forward and stared directly at Mandy Smith.

'I'm almost completely recovered now, Mandy. You saved my life, and I'll never forget that. No one has ever helped me like you have.'

His intensity unnerved her and she looked toward the floor. 'That's very kind of you, Hank,' she said. 'I only did what I had to do.'

'You didn't have to do all you've done. You're a fine woman. Any man who had you as his wife would be a very lucky feller.'

'Hank, I—'

'Please, Mandy – just listen,' he said. He rose and crossed the room to where she sat. He knelt and took one of her hands in his. 'I'm going to leave here tomorrow night. I have things I need to do. If everything goes my way, I'll make it out alive. And if I do, I will come back for you.'

Tears pooled in her eyes. 'What are you going to do, Hank? Are you going to kill Ted Flynn?'

'That's not my plan. But if Ted gets in the way, he'll wish he hadn't.'

'I don't care about Ted,' Mandy noted. 'I just don't want you to be hurt.'

'I'm going to be careful. I'm playing to win.'

'I know, Hank. I would like for us to . . . be together.'

He smiled, and his features softened. 'That's all I needed to hear,' he said.

He kissed her hand and she rose. All the emotions that had been building in the weeks since he had returned to Eugene burst forth. He lifted her in his arms and carried her to the bed.

CHAPTER FOUR

The first crimson light of dawn streamed through the curtains, and Hank Chesham was already awake. Mandy lay beside him, her head on his shoulder. She was sound asleep.

Tonight he would leave. He would have Mandy get his horse and then he would ride out. He had a plan, although it was still a vague one. It was all he had.

He was going to take the fight to Ted Flynn.

Chesham moved slightly and Mandy stirred. She lifted her face and looked at him.

'Have you gotten any sleep?' she asked.

'Not much,' he said. 'But enough.'

'What are you going to do when you leave?'

'You remember my Aunt Tillie? She died not long before I left for New Mexico.'

'I remember her.'

'She lived in a little cabin out past the Rimrock.'

'I don't think I ever went there. Is it still standing?'

He nodded. 'Yes, it is. I rode past it on my way to the ranch. It's still there, and it's in pretty good shape.'

'Are you going there?'

'Yes. I don't think anyone's been out there in years. It'll be the perfect place for me to stay while I do what I need to do.'

In the afternoon, Mandy closed the café for a couple of hours and went out to procure some items for Chesham. She returned with two bulging sacks and a rectangular cardboard box under her arm. Inside the sacks were various food provisions and a medium-sized wooden box with the word 'DANGER!' stamped across the top.

Chesham took the box and examined it. Inside were five sticks of dynamite. He looked toward Mandy and raised an eyebrow.

'What did the old man at the hardware store say when you bought this?' he asked.

'I told you he wouldn't ask any questions. He was a good friend of my pa's. He took me back in the office and put it in a bag so no one could see me buy it. The only thing he said was, 'Be careful with this, honey.'

Chesham grinned. He knew Mandy was one of the best-liked women in Eugene. When he had discussed the items he would need, she had guaranteed her ability to acquire them. It had been no idle promise.

Mandy placed the cardboard box on the bed. Chesham opened it and withdrew a beautiful new Winchester rifle from inside. Two boxes of shells were in one of the sacks.

'This is all I'm going to need,' said Chesham.

Mandy re-opened the café and worked until the early evening. It was a little after ten o'clock when she brought Chesham's horse to the alley behind the café. The night was pitch black and drizzly.

She tapped quietly on the back door, holding the horse's reins with her other hand. Chesham opened the door and stepped out, holding a couple sacks of provisions that Mandy had prepared for him. The horse recognized him and whickered as he reached out and patted it on the neck.

'I think she's missed you,' said Mandy with a grin.

'I've missed her, too,' said Chesham.

He no longer had the saddle-bags he had been carrying when he was attacked. Along with the paper he had forced Ted and Phoebe Flynn to sign, they had been taken by the three men who had left him for dead. He was happy to see that his saddle had been well cared-for by the old man at the stable. He had tied the two sacks together with a rope, which he wrapped around the saddlehorn. He slid his new rifle into the scabbard, then took the reins from Mandy and put an arm around her, pulling her close to him.

'I will be back for you soon,' he said.

'How long?'

'A week – ten days, maybe.'

'What if I can't wait that long and I come out to see you?'

He frowned. 'You have to promise you won't do that. You might get hurt. Those men who work for Ted wouldn't hesitate to kill a woman.'

'I won't come out there. I don't even really know where it is.'

'I'm sure there'll be news in town within a day or two. I'm going to get people's attention.'

He kissed her, and she stepped into the doorway as he climbed into the saddle. She lifted a hand and he tipped his hat to her, then rode down the alley toward the hills at the south end of town.

Chesham pulled his hat down low, although he doubted anyone would recognize him even in broad daylight. His beard was much longer now than when he had ridden into town nearly three weeks before. There were almost no people out on the streets this late anyway.

He rode through an upper-class residential district and then turned east, heading across the river to Springfield. His horse's hoofs made clopping noises on the boards as he crossed the bridge. Once in Springfield, he kept to the south, skirting the town. He kept off the main trails, staying within the forested hills. It took him nearly two hours before he heeled his sorrel down an incline and pulled leather in front of his late aunt's cabin. It was in an isolated, forested gully, about five miles south of the Rimrock. Chesham saw no signs of recent human activity in the area, which didn't surprise him. Few people even knew the place existed, and it would be almost impossible to find unless one knew exactly where to look.

He tied his horse to a post in front of the cabin and pushed the door open. As he stepped into the small house, memories flooded back to him. His Aunt Tillie had been his mother's sister, and she had been widowed early. For three decades she had lived alone in this little shack, rarely going into town and associating almost exclusively with the members of her extended family. He could remember spending time out here in his childhood, fishing with his father in the nearby river and then bringing home their catches for his mother and Aunt Tillie to fry up. He had always kept in close touch with Tillie, and when she died he had inherited the fifty acres on which the cabin stood. It was evident that no one had taken an interest in the place during his absence in New Mexico. Most people didn't even know it was there.

There was a multitude of cobwebs and rodent droppings, but the roof wasn't leaking and the wood stove was in good shape.

Chesham went out and brought his horse around to the lean-to behind the cabin. He took the sacks that Mandy had prepared for him and went back into the shack. He stripped the blanket off the bed and replaced it with one from the sacks. He took out some jerky, hard tack, and tins of fruit. He ate some of the hard tack, thinking over his next move. Then he stepped back out and checked the loads in his Navy Colt. The clouds had dispersed and the moonlight had fully emerged now, illuminating the trees around him.

By this time tomorrow, he thought, Ted Flynn ain't going to know what hit him.

Shortly after dawn, Chesham retrieved his sorrel and rode east, again taking care to avoid any established trails. He knew this land like the back of his hand and could have found his way around with his eyes closed.

Chesham was heading for Ted Flynn's ranch, the Double F. It was situated in a valley adjacent to the Rimrock, separated by several tree-cloaked foothills. Chesham rode around the south end of the Double F and dismounted, climbing a small rise and kneeling between two massive fir trees. He raised his field glasses to his eyes and surveyed Flynn's ranch.

There was mist covering the pastures as the rising sun crept above the distant ridges. Chesham gritted his teeth as he looked over the ranch.

Ted Flynn had inherited the Double F from his father and his uncle, who had owned the ranch as partners. It had always been a well-run establishment, but now it was a massive operation, even bigger than the Rimrock. Chesham figured there were at least six or seven hundred cattle there, as well as a few hundred horses. A handful of cowpunchers were visible far out in the fields, watching the cattle. The bunkhouse was at least twice the size that it had been when Chesham had left for New Mexico, and, just like at the Rimrock, the main house had been considerably expanded.

Chesham wondered how much of the profits from the Rimrock had been used on the Double F. Or how much of the seven thousand dollars he had inherited from his brother and sent back up to the bank in Eugene. The treachery of Ted and Phoebe Flynn was still almost beyond his comprehension.

The house was in darkness, and a small trickle of smoke rose from the chimney on the bunkhouse. He wondered how often Ted and Phoebe used the house here; it seemed they spent most of their time at the Rimrock. He took another look at the house, and noticed the large, tidy woodpile at the back. The woodpile had a roof over it to keep it dry.

Chesham smiled thinly and pushed himself to his feet. The woodpile would come in handy later.

The door to the bunkhouse burst open and two men emerged into the yard. They lighted cigars and stood talking by the trough. Chesham's pulse quickened when he recognized one of them as the man with the hickory stick who had delivered the most brutal blows in the alley a few weeks ago.

He had had no doubt that Ted Flynn had been behind the attempted murder, but seeing the bushwhacker coming out of Flynn's bunkhouse still came as something of a shock. He knew now that Flynn assumed he had been killed in that alley. Otherwise, he would have sent his henchman on their way to protect himself.

Chesham studied the man closely. He was big, with a deeply lined face and broad shoulders. His bulky frame moved with an unexpected agility as the man paced back and forth near the bunkhouse door, talking animatedly to the other man, whom Chesham didn't recognize. There was a cruelty evident in the big man's face – mostly in his thin-lipped mouth. That cruelty had burst forth in the alley. The man's taunting words as he beat Chesham with the stick reverberated in the latter's mind.

I don't know your name, feller, thought Chesham. But we're going to meet again, real soon. And I'm going to get my pound of flesh.

He took his attention away from the man outside the bunkhouse and looked beyond the main house toward the well. It was still exactly where it had been years before, although it looked bigger. That made sense, given how much the Double F had expanded over the last five years.

He scanned the fields and the layout of the buildings one more time, then climbed back down the rise, retrieved his horse, and rode back to the cabin.

Chesham spent the rest of the day clearing out his temporary home and preparing for the activities he had planned for the night.

He found a broom under the bed and swept out the cabin. He left the front and back doors open as he went down to the river and fetched water. When he got back, he ate some beans and cold beef that Mandy had packed for him. He sat on the edge of the bed and thought of her. He didn't underestimate the danger of what he was about to undertake, but the thought of being with Mandy filled him with determination and even, for the first time in years, a sense of hope.

He slept for a couple hours in the late afternoon, awakening as dusk settled into the sky. He cleaned and oiled his Navy Colt, then repeated the process with his Winchester rifle. Finally, he loaded the rifle, saddled his horse, and rode out of the valley, taking his time as he traversed the folded hills and gullies on his way to the Double F. The sky was dark and overcast by the time he drew reins and then picketed his mount behind the same small rise at the rear of Flynn's ranch where he had surveyed the property earlier that day.

Chesham used his field glasses to look over the ranch again. There were horsemen in the fields, far from the house. He would be able to carry out his tasks unobserved by them. The aroma of food drifted on the wind from the bunkhouse, which was about a hundred yards from Chesham's position. After supper, the crew would be settling in for the night. He looked toward the house and, as before, observed no signs of activity there. Most of the curtains were drawn and there was no one moving about inside.

He descended the back of the rise and removed a length of rope and two sticks of dynamite from one of the sacks tied to the saddlehorn. He left the horse and walked east through the trees toward the well. He halted behind a giant maple tree and took a careful look around.

Apart from a cow standing near the fence beyond the well, Chesham was alone in this corner of the Double F. He crouched and moved swiftly across the grass to the well. As he had noted earlier, it had been expanded considerably. He looped his rope around it and tied it carefully, leaving just enough slack to insert a stick of dynamite on the north side and then the south side of the well. When he was finished, he looked out toward the fields to see if he had been spotted, but the distant riders were oblivious to him. The cow regarded him without interest.

Chesham moved back into the trees and walked until he was directly behind the main house. He dashed from the trees to the back of the house, palming his pistol as he did so. He stopped on the back porch, standing perfectly still as he leaned his head to the side and peered into the house through one of the large windows beside the door.

Most of the furniture inside was covered. It was clear that Ted and Phoebe used the Rimrock as their primary residence. The door was locked. Chesham used the butt of his pistol to break a small window in the back door, and then reached through to open it. He stepped into the dark house and made his way past the kitchen into the hallway that led to the front rooms. He passed the dining room, his gun still in his hand. The door to Ted Flynn's office was ajar. Chesham pushed it open and entered the room.

The blinds were drawn over the windows, so Chesham closed the door behind him and struck a match. A lantern stood on the mantle of the fireplace, and he lighted it, careful to keep the wick turned down very low. He moved to the desk and sat down. There were no papers on the top of the desk. He opened every drawer, but found nothing of interest in them. After a few minutes, he extinguished the lantern and walked back out to the porch.

A small stable stood about ten yards from the back porch. This was where Flynn used to keep his personal mounts; the main stable was located over near the bunkhouse. Chesham crossed the dewy grass to the small stable and pulled the front door open slightly. He stepped inside and closed the door behind him, then struck a match and looked around. There were only three stalls in this stable. The stalls were empty, and Chesham assumed Flynn's horses were being kept at the Rimrock.

On a table at the back were four kerosene lamps, neatly arranged in a row. Chesham lighted one with his match, again making sure to keep the wick turned down. He was preparing to light the others when he heard a sound behind him. He drew his pistol and moved into the shadows of the nearest stall, his eyes riveted to the stable door.

He heard approaching footsteps. They terminated outside the door, and someone pushed the door open very slowly. Chesham could see the silhouette of a man in the doorway, and then the man stepped into the stable. He wore long johns with cowboy boots. In his right hand was a thick hickory stick.

CHAPTER FIVE

The man's rheumy eyes flicked over the stable. He looked drunk.

'I know someone's hiding in here,' he said. 'I was going to take a piss and I saw a light. Come on out or you're going to get hurt.'

Chesham tensed. He was crouched in the stall, watching the man with the stick through a gap in the boards, his breathing silent. Every fiber of his body was alive with the danger of the moment. He slipped his Colt back into its holster.

'Come on, now,' the man repeated. He started walking forward, his gaze fixed on the dim lantern. 'You the same boy that stole that saddle from here a few months back?' He slapped the stick against his open palm. 'Don't make me give you another whipping, kid.'

The man passed the first stall and looked into it. He continued on to the second stall, swinging the stick menacingly.

'All right, then,' he said. 'I guess we're going to do this the hard way.'

His shadow fell across the opening of the stall in which Chesham knelt. He squinted as he looked toward the stall, and before he could defend himself, Chesham burst forward. His fingers gripped the man's throat and he lifted him off the ground, thrusting him back into a post across from the stall. The impact was savage, and the man dropped his stick and reached up, desperately trying to pry Chesham's fingers from his throat.

Hank Chesham leaned in close to the man's face. 'Remember me?' he asked. 'Bet you thought you'd never see me again.'

His fingers tightened, and the man's eyes bulged. He gasped, trying to breathe, and spittle flew from his mouth on to Chesham's sleeve. Stark fear was etched on his face.

'You're – dead—' the man managed to mutter.

'Not yet,' said Chesham. 'I'm going to take care of you, and then I'm going to find your two pals. Where are they – here or at the Rimrock?'

The man sputtered, as if trying to answer Chesham's question. Chesham relaxed his grip very slightly, trying to make out what the man was saying. Suddenly the man thrust his thumb into Chesham's eye, in a quick stabbing motion. A searing pain burst through Chesham's eyeball and the socket around it, and he released the man, stepping back and clutching his head.

The man grabbed his stick and moved in, cracking Chesham hard in the ribs. Chesham fell back, seemingly incapacitated, and again the stick swung toward him. Chesham reacted with startling speed, moving in close to the man and grasping his arm. He smashed an elbow into the man's face and twisted his arm behind him, pulling it up sharply behind his back. The man cried out, dropping the stick.

Chesham was consumed by rage. He pulled the arm with all his strength and the man squealed, just before the arm broke with an audible snap. The man's knees buckled and he fell forward on to the dirt floor. He was only unconscious for a moment, and then, groaning, he rolled over on to his back, clutching his broken arm. Tears streaked down his face and he tried to push himself to his feet.

Chesham now picked up the hickory stick. In one graceful motion, he brought it down across the man's temple. Bones crunched and the skin split, spraying blood on to the wall behind them. The man's eyes rolled back and he lay motionless.

Chesham leaned against the wall of the stall, panting. He fingered his injured eye gingerly. It was swelling, but he didn't have trouble seeing. He walked to the door of the stable and looked out across the misty grass toward the bunkhouse. There was no indication that anyone inside had heard the fight.

He returned to the rear of the stable and lighted the other three lamps. He looked down at the man on the ground and nudged him with the toe of his boot. The side of the man's head was now grotesquely swollen. He didn't appear to be breathing. Chesham leaned down and felt his chest. His heart was no longer beating.

Chesham carried the four now-burning lamps and set them down on the ground near the door. He picked up one of them and turned the wick all the way up. He tossed it into the middle stall. The glass shattered and the burning kerosene exploded on the dry straw. Within seconds, flames were licking up the wall toward the ceiling.

Chesham cast one final look at the dead man at the back.

'Welcome to hell,' he said.

Carrying the lanterns, he exited the stable and ran across the grass to the back porch. He turned up a lamp and threw it at the woodpile, which immediately burst into flames. Turning up another lamp, he kicked open the back door of Ted Flynn's house. He trotted down to the parlor and hurled the third lamp against the wall. The lamp burst and the wall was engulfed in fire, the lace curtains curling in the flames.

He ran back out to the porch and into the yard. He changed course and went toward the bunkhouse. The fires hadn't attracted any attention yet and there were no lights on inside. Chesham reached the back of the structure and, turning up the last lantern to its full capacity, he stood ten feet from the wall and threw the lantern at it. Seconds later, the entire rear wall was aflame.

Chesham raced back to the yard behind the main house. He drew his pistol and fired three shots into the air. He had no desire to kill the people in the bunkhouse, but he wanted to be sure the various fires were uncontainable before the men could begin fighting them. Smoke was now billowing out of the house and the stable, and the woodpile was consumed by a roaring fire.

Chesham ran past the small stable and headed across the field toward the well. He could see horsemen riding in from the pastures, but their view of him was blocked by the smoke. Chest heaving, he reached the well and knelt beside it, removing two matches from his shirt pocket. He lighted the fuse on the first stick of dynamite, then quickly ran around and lighted the second one. With the sound of the hissing fuses burning in his ears, he made for the trees at the south side of the pasture. He had just reached the rim of maples and firs when the dynamite blew, two loud explosions utterly demolishing the well and sending large stones into it. There would be no way for the men to get water there. There would be no way to stop the near-total destruction of the Double F ranch.

Chesham moved into the trees and then turned to his right, in the direction of the foothill behind which he had picketed his horse. In less than two minutes he was there. He grabbed his field glasses, clambered up the back of the rise, and knelt between the two big maple trees at the top. His lips spread into a tight smile as he surveyed the chaos before him.

The small stable was blazing uncontrollably. The north and east sides of the main house were burning, and Chesham could hear glass shatter as the heat burst the windows. The flames were climbing inexorably to the roof. Within an hour, the entire house would be a charred ruin.

He looked toward the bunkhouse. It, too, was beyond any hope of being salvaged, even if the well had been in working order. Flames danced along the entire length of the roof. At least a dozen men stood in the yard in various states of dress; Chesham's decision to fire the shots before blowing up the well had kept anyone from dying in the bunkhouse fire.

He heard shouts to his right and fixed the field glasses on three horsemen who were riding back from the location of the well. They were yelling and gesticulating in bewilderment. Everyone now knew that the well had been destroyed.

He took in the scene for a few minutes before returning to his horse and departing for the cabin.

*

Tendrils of smoke still drifted up from the burnt remains of the Double F as Ted Flynn dismounted and examined the destruction in the early morning light. Apart from the large main stable and the cook shack, every significant building on the ranch had been burnt to the ground.

Flynn had been staying in Eugene when word reached him that someone had destroyed the ranch that he had inherited from his father and his uncle. He had ridden in with two of his most reliable lieutenants, Don Rowland and Al King. They sat their horses a few yards behind their boss. Jack Masterton, the ramrod of the Double F, was nowhere to be seen, and the rider who had gone to town to fetch Flynn had mentioned that Masterton hadn't been seen since the night before. His hickory stick was missing, too.

Don Rowland shifted in the saddle, struggling to make sense of what he was seeing. 'Lord Almighty,' he said. 'Whoever done this did a real thorough job.'

Flynn pivoted, his eyes blazing. 'Shut your mouth, Don. If you'd have done your job right in that alley a few weeks ago, my ranch would still be standing.'

Rowland's face was pale as Flynn spoke. 'What you mean by that, boss?' he asked weakly.

'You worthless fool,' Flynn snarled. He looked at Al King, whose analytical capacity was marginally more advanced than that of Rowland. 'You know what I'm saying, Al?'

76

King nodded. 'Yes, sir. You're saying it was Hank Chesham who done this.'

'That's right,' said Flynn bitterly. 'Hank Chesham.'

'I don't see how it could be him,' Rowland said.

'You don't see a lot of things, Don.'

'Boss, if you'd have seen the state he was in when we left him in that alley, you'd know what I mean. There's no way he could have survived that. He was barely breathing.'

'Well, "barely" is enough, it appears.' Flynn shook his head. 'I should have known better than to have ranch hands do a job like that. I should have found myself a real killer and paid him good money. At least I would know the job had been done right.'

Rowland and King were silent. They knew this wasn't the time to argue with Ted Flynn. The only reason they hadn't shot Chesham that night was because it was too risky, given the dense population in that area of Eugene. Someone would have been bound to hear the shot and come to find out what the commotion was. But Flynn wouldn't listen to reason at the moment. And as they examined the burned buildings before them, neither Rowland nor King could blame him.

'You boys go check out that well,' Flynn said.

The two men exchanged glances, then rode away to obey Flynn's command. Leading his horse by the reins, Flynn walked forward and stopped near what was left of his house. The Double F crew stood near the cook shack, waiting for their breakfast. There wasn't really much else for them to do at the moment.

So Chesham's alive, thought Flynn. And he's made good on his promise. I knew he would, as long as he was still breathing.

Marrying Phoebe and taking over the Rimrock had enabled Flynn to turn the Double F into one of the largest and most efficient ranching operations in the southern Willamette Valley. Four thousand dollars of Chesham's dead brother's money had helped, too. With both ranches in his name, Flynn was a name to be reckoned with, regardless of the distaste that others felt for him after he married Phoebe. The opinions of others were no longer of any concern to him.

But now the situation had changed, suddenly and most drastically. He knew Hank Chesham well, and he knew what sort of man he was. Otherwise, he would never have sent those men into Eugene to eliminate him. Flynn didn't think of himself as a violent man, only as one who would do whatever had to be done to maintain his position. By failing to kill Chesham, Rowland, King, and Masterton had enabled the man to recuperate and unleash his vengeance on Ted Flynn. The entire thing was now out of hand, and out of Flynn's control. He knew there would be no stopping Chesham unless he was somehow able to locate him and kill him himself.

78

This was a job he now knew he couldn't leave to others.

The sound of approaching hoofbeats distracted Flynn from his thoughts. He turned around and saw Phoebe riding toward him. She drew reins a few feet from him and dismounted. He walked toward her and put his arm around her shoulders. Her face was anxious as she took in what remained of the Double F.

'My goodness, Ted,' she said. 'How did this happen?'

Flynn exhaled slowly, considering his words.

'These weren't accidental fires,' he said. 'Hank did this.'

She raised her head and met his eyes. 'Hank?' she asked. 'You're sure?'

Flynn nodded. 'It's Hank. I guarantee it. He burned down the house, the little stable, and the bunkhouse. He dynamited the well, too.'

'Lord help us, Tim. What are we going to do?'

'My men and I are going to find him,' said Flynn, in a tone that sounded more confident than he felt. 'Then we're going to kill him.'

Phoebe's chin trembled. 'Kill him? What are you talking about, Ted?'

'He's gone too far now, and he's not finished. This won't be over until either Hank Chesham is dead, or I am.'

'You think he wants you dead?'

Flynn's gaze was frank. 'Can you blame him, Phoebe?'

She was silent for several moments. 'Maybe we should just give him the Rimrock.'

'You can't be serious!'

'What if he kills you, Ted? Have you thought of that?'

'Of course I have.'

'Aren't you a little afraid that he might?'

'No, damn it, I'm not!'

Phoebe put her hands over her face, trying to calm her nerves.

'I'm sorry, Ted. I just don't know what to do. I can't sleep, I can't eat. . . .'

'I know,' said Flynn. 'I'm sorry. This is a god-damned mess. But I'm going to take care of everything. Don't you worry. It might take a little time, but I'm going to find him and finish this.'

CHAPTER SIX

Hank Chesham badly wanted a cigarette, but he knew it was too dangerous, so he refrained. He was standing in the shadows behind Ted Flynn's general store in Springfield and, although it was after midnight and the streets were virtually empty, he didn't want to attract unwanted attention.

He stood quietly, his senses sharp. He knew that Flynn wasn't a stupid man; it was quite possible that he had a man inside the store, lying in wait in case Chesham came to wreak more havoc.

His appearance was so vastly different from what it had been before he left for New Mexico that he wasn't worried about being recognized. He had ridden by the front of the store before riding around the block to the alley. There had been no one inside. After ten minutes of standing at the back door, he decided to go in.

He slammed his right shoulder against the door and it gave instantly. He paused to listen again, but,

81

hearing nothing, he stepped into the rear room of the store, closing the door behind him. He thumb-snapped a vesta and looked around. He was in a storage room. To his right were various barrels and boxes; to his left were shelves stocked with tins, bags of beans, and other food items.

Chesham moved forward and opened a door that led into a hallway. Up ahead he could see the counter and, beyond that, the front room of the store. Halfway down the hallway was a closed door. He approached it and twisted the knob. The door wasn't locked. Beyond the door was an office. Chesham had extinguished the first match and now lighted another. There was a lantern on the desk and he lighted it after sitting in the plush leather chair.

As he had done in Flynn's office at the Double F, Chesham went through each of the desk drawers. He wasn't entirely sure about what he was looking for, but he had a nagging feeling that Flynn might have some incriminating documents – documents that would prove valuable down the road. There was nothing to be found in the drawers here except financial records and inventories for the store.

Voices from the street out front drew Chesham's attention. He rose and leaned his head into the doorway, looking toward the windows at the front of the store. A couple of drunks from the saloon down the street were talking loudly, their raucous laughter reverberating through the night. Chesham watched them for a few moments, until they turned and walked up the sidewalk. Their voices faded as they turned down a side street.

Chesham walked toward the front room and looked around. It was a very large store, with almost everything a person could possibly want on its shelves or displayed on racks. Women's hats, jugs of molasses, fancy watches, tins of sardines – all neatly arranged for Ted Flynn's profit.

Yes, thought Chesham. Ted's really done well for himself. He won't have any trouble replacing all this.

He returned to the back room and removed a can of coal oil from a shelf. He opened it and dumped some of the liquid on to the floor, then poured a stream of it in the hallway. He went back into the office and poured it on to the desk. He tossed a lighted match on to it, and another in the store room before he exited through the back. As he mounted his horse in the alley, he could already see the flames rising through the window of the back door.

He sat his horse for a couple of minutes before firing shots into the night and riding out into the darkness.

Ted Flynn filled his pipe and lighted a match, stirring the flame over the tobacco. A thick plume of smoke rose into the air over his desk. He blew out the match and looked through the smoke at the two men standing across from him.

83

'What's the word on the store, boys?' he asked.

'Pretty much everything is gone,' said Al King. 'Anything that wasn't burned was ruined when they put out the fire. Also, the smoke destroyed a lot of things.'

'It's going to cost a lot of money to rebuild it. Maybe more than it's worth.'

'The fire would have spread to the buildings next door if he hadn't fired those shots,' King observed. 'They were barely able to put it out – it was blazing real good.'

'The bastard is crazy. He's out of his mind.' Flynn stared past King to a point on the wall. 'I should have had someone on guard duty there,' he said quietly.

'I'll make it happen,' said Don Rowland. 'Starting tonight.'

'And put someone at the boarding house, too. I want riders with guns on duty here at the Rimrock – at least five of them.' The two men nodded. Flynn sat back in his chair and brushed some stray flecks of tobacco off his shirt. 'Now we have to consider our next move. We can't sit around waiting for Chesham. We've got to find him.'

'You have any idea where he might be hiding, boss?' asked King.

Flynn shook his head. 'No idea at all,' he said. 'That's why I want you, Don, to get some men together and take to the hills. I want y'all to check every gully, every box canyon – everything. Take some provisions – it should take you at least two days to do a thorough job. If he is hiding in the hills, then the only place he could be is south of here.' He glanced at King. 'You're going to be in charge of security here at the ranch, and in town.'

'I'll see to it,' King said.

'How did he even know I own the store? I didn't own it when he went away to New Mexico. Someone is giving him information.'

'Who would do that?' asked Rowland.

'I don't know. But when we get our hands on Hank Chesham, we're going to ask him some real hard questions. We're going to find out who's been helping him. Whoever it is, they're going to pay.'

'So you want him taken alive, no matter what?'

Flynn drew on his pipe before answering. 'I would prefer taking him alive. There are things I want to know. But if he won't come willingly and the only thing you can do is shoot him then . . . go ahead and kill him.'

From the top of the cliff above the Rimrock ranch, Hank Chesham watched Ted Flynn walk out into the front yard before the main house. Two men were with him. Although he didn't know their names, Chesham recognized them instantly. They were the other two men who had tried to kill him in the alley.

He watched them interact with Flynn. He seemed to be giving them directions, pointing to the hills on the south side of the ranch. Chesham moved a little further back from the edge of the cliff, not wanting to take the risk of sunlight reflecting off the lenses of his field glasses and giving away his position.

Flynn finished talking and strode back into the house. The two men spoke to each other for another minute or two, then walked over to the bunkhouse. When they didn't emerge after ten minutes, Chesham moved away from the cliff and fetched his horse from the trees. He descended the back of the small mountain and rode through the forest toward his cabin.

He realized he still didn't know how he was going to finish all this. He had been so focused on hurting Ted Flynn that he had almost forgotten about the Rimrock. In the end, that was what mattered. But how could he force Flynn to give it back, legally? He decided to cross that bridge when he came to it. The only thing he could do would be to continue to inflict damage on Flynn until the man sought to negotiate. Flynn was totally ruthless; he was the sort of man who only respected force. He had no shame about what he had done.

Killing Flynn would only turn the ranch over to Phoebe, and Chesham knew he couldn't kill her. Perhaps he could make her sign it over if Flynn were dead. Certainly Flynn had crossed the ultimate line when he sent the men to kill Chesham. There would be no quarter now.

Chesham picked his way through the trees, pushing branches aside as he followed trails that only he knew. The time had come for caution. If he were to attack the boarding house tonight, Flynn would almost certainly have men waiting for him. Chesham decided he would wait a few days before he struck again.

CHAPTER SEVEN

Three nights later, Chesham rode into Eugene a little after midnight. The darkness was frigid, and a pale moon was barely visible behind a thick blanket of clouds. A drizzling rain fell, having beleaguered Chesham since he rode out from the cabin nearly two hours before.

Chesham drew reins in a dark, muddy alley behind the darkened millinery a couple blocks away from the boarding house. Across the alley from where he sat his sorrel there was a large, shadowy back yard, and none of the windows in the house showed light. Chesham led his horse into the yard and picketed it there behind a large laurel bush. He returned to the alley and began making his way through the mud toward the rear of the boarding house.

As he passed the back of a saloon a block before his destination, Chesham saw an elderly drunk urinating in the alley. He recognized the old man from many years before, although he couldn't recall his name. The man looked at Chesham with bleary eyes and nodded in acknowledgment as he passed by. It was evident that he didn't recognize Chesham, although that was no doubt in part due to the man's extreme intoxication. But it further confirmed Chesham's belief that his appearance had changed drastically in the years since he went to New Mexico.

He pulled up the collar of his sheepskin and turned left when the alley hit A Street. He stepped on to the plank sidewalk and made his way up to Main. He halted on the corner under a street lamp. There were three saloons within the nearest two blocks, and they were the only buildings that showed any signs of life. To his right he could see a lantern burning above the door of the boarding house.

A large man stood next to the door, cupping a hand around a match as he lighted a cheroot. Chesham recognized him as one of the men from the bunkhouse at the Double F. So Flynn had done exactly what Chesham had thought he would do. He was expecting another attack and had now taken to posting guards at his businesses.

Chesham backed into a nearby doorway. The man outside the boarding house hadn't noticed him. Several minutes passed as Chesham watched to see if there were any signs of other guards. The guard stayed where he was, smoking another cigarette and staring idly into the street, obviously bored.

From the other side of the boarding house, a few men emerged from a saloon. They spotted the guard and greeted him loudly. He waved back and they began to walk toward him. The men were clearly drunk and their voices carried to where Chesham was standing.

'Hey, Jake,' one of the men said to the guard. 'You got the watch tonight, huh?'

Jake smiled sardonically. 'Yep. Guess it was just my lucky night.'

The men laughed. 'Any sign of that feller? What's his name?'

'Chesham,' said Jake. 'And there ain't been no sign of him tonight, just like there ain't been any sign of him for the last three nights. I'm starting to wonder if he doesn't know that Mr. Flynn owns this place.'

One of the men belched loudly and scratched at his ample belly. 'Hell, you got time for a beer or two, Jake? I don't think I'm quite done drinking for the night.'

'Well, I'd like to, boys, but I don't think I should,' Jake said regretfully.

'Aw, come on, now. If he ain't come yet, he probably ain't coming at all. It'll only be five or ten minutes. I'll buy you a shot of rye to warm you up.' The drunken cowpunch rubbed his hands up and down his arms. 'It's cold as hell out tonight.'

'Yeah, you got time, Jake. Ain't nothing going to

happen while you're gone.'

Jake was silent for a moment, thinking about how nice a couple beers and a shot of whiskey sounded. He sighed loudly, sweeping his eyes around the street again as if to reassure himself that Chesham wasn't coming tonight.

Presently, he said: 'Hell, you fellers are right. He ain't coming. Let's go wet our whistles a little.'

The two men roared their approval, slapping Jake heartily on the back. He turned and walked with them up the sidewalk to the saloon. They shouldered through the batwings and disappeared from Chesham's sight. He emerged from the shadowed doorway and crossed the street, making his way quickly to the door of the boarding house.

Through the front window, he could see into the lobby. There was a carpeted stairway to the left and, beneath the upstairs landing, a registration desk. An old woman came from behind the desk and walked to the bottom of the stairs. She called something up the stairs, and Chesham heard a voice respond. The woman slowly began to climb the stairs, oblivious to Chesham's presence by the front door.

The woman reached the landing and went into one of the rooms. Chesham slipped into the lobby and crossed to the desk. There was nothing of interest to him there, so he went on into the hallway behind the desk. Three doors led off the hallway, which terminated in a door leading into the back alley. Chesham tried the first door; it led into a small bedroom, tidily kept and obviously unoccupied. Chesham wondered if Ted Flynn ever used it when he was in town.

He went on to the second door, behind which was a laundry room with neatly folded sheets and blankets on shelves above a large washing tub. Several pillows were stacked against the far wall. Chesham went out and stopped outside the third door. When he opened it, he found what he had been looking for. There was a large oak desk and the exact kind of plush leather chairs that Chesham knew Ted Flynn favored. He stepped in and closed the door behind him.

The curtains were drawn, but there was light coming in from the saloon next door. Chesham crossed the room and parted the curtains just enough for him to see better. He sat down at the desk and pulled open the wide top drawer beneath the blotter. There were two stacks of letters there, each tied with a string. He pulled out the first stack and held it up to the light streaming through the window.

As he read the elegant scrawl on the top envelope, his insides turned cold. 'I'll be goddamned,' he said under his breath.

It was a letter from Judge Ray Owens of Santa Fe, New Mexico. The man who had tried and convicted him after he had been falsely accused of robbing that stage outside town. What in the hell had Judge

Owens been doing writing letters to Ted Flynn?

Chesham removed a small folding knife from his pocket and cut the string that held the letters together. He opened the top envelope and read the letter, which was short and rather cryptic.

It read:

Dear Mr. Flynn – Thank you for your telegram and the information about the prisoner. I read it with great interest. I am pleased to accept your generous offer. I will send you more information soon about where you can send the funds. You will be pleased to know that a conviction is certain, given the evidence against him. The wheels of justice turn swiftly and surely. Yours sincerely, Ray Owens, Attorney-at-law and Justice of the Peace, Santa Fe.

Questions raced through Chesham's mind, but the answers were all there in the letter. What possible explanation could there be for such a correspondence if Ted Flynn hadn't paid off Judge Owens in order to put Chesham in prison?

Chesham had known Owens was corrupt from the first day of the trial, when the judge had ruled against every request and motion that the defense attorney had made. Chesham had already figured that Owens was one of those law officers who believed the accused were automatically guilty. He had never imagined that Ted Flynn could be behind his imprisonment.

He opened the other two letters that Owens had sent to Flynn. The first included bank information for the money Flynn had promised. The third acknowledged the receipt of the money and informed Flynn that Chesham had been convicted of the hold-up and sent to the Pile.

Chesham placed the letters back in the envelopes and put them in the inside pocket of his sheepskin. His mind reeled and, at last, he understood why Judge Owens had released him and given him money when he died. The crooked old man had had an attack of conscience in the final twilight before he met his maker. He wondered bitterly how many other people had been sent into the hell of the Santa Fe prison because of Judge Owens' corruption.

Had Flynn set the entire thing up, including the phony robbery charges? Chesham dismissed the idea. There was no way he could have arranged the robbery as well as the subsequent trial. Chesham had sent a telegram to Phoebe after his arrest. It must have been then that Flynn saw his opportunity and decided to pay off the judge. Flynn had connections all over the southwest, and he wouldn't have had much trouble learning that Owens was crooked.

What did Phoebe know? Her betrayal had been so deep that Chesham would put little past her. However, he reckoned that Flynn would have kept the information from Phoebe if he could. One way or another, Chesham intended to find out before he was through.

He picked up the other stack of letters from the drawer and a deep anger overtook him. He slit the string with his knife and quickly flicked through the envelopes, scanning the writing on them. It was his own handwriting, and there were six letters – all the letters he had sent to Phoebe at the Rimrock during his first year in prison. None of them had been opened. His eyes were like chips of ice as he looked at them. He placed them in his pocket with the others.

He sat motionless in the chair for a few minutes. Then a voice from the lobby caught his attention, and he was instantly on his feet, his hand reaching down toward the pistol on his hip.

It was a woman's voice, and he recognized it as that of the old woman he had seen in the lobby a few minutes before. He moved toward the door and pressed his ear against it.

'Mr Jake, come here,' she said. 'The door to the laundry room is open. It wasn't open when I went upstairs.'

Chesham heard the front door of the boarding house close and he cursed his own carelessness.

'You sure about that, miss?' The voice was Jake's.

'Yes, I am,' she replied a little impatiently. 'I never leave that door open.'

Booted footsteps approached the hallway. 'All

right, then,' Jake said, his voice a little slurred after his visit to the saloon. 'You have a seat here and I'll take a look around.'

Chesham moved behind the door. He decided not to use his pistol unless he had to. He removed his knife from his boot and held his breath unconsciously as he listened to Jake come down the hall.

He heard him enter the laundry room and then return to the hallway after a few moments.

'There ain't nobody in there, ma'am,' Jake said as he closed the laundry room door. Footsteps moved back toward the lobby, and then stopped abruptly.

'Please check the other rooms,' the woman said. 'He might be hiding in one of them.'

'All right, I will.'

Jake was now clearly irritated by her and her requests. Chesham listened as he went into the small bedroom and exited after a few seconds.

'Nobody in the bedroom,' he called. 'I'll check the office.'

His boots reverberated as he approached the room where Chesham lurked. His hand gripped the doorknob and pushed the door open. He stepped in and looked around, first toward the desk and then across toward the parted curtains. He frowned and stepped in a little further, pushing the door closed to look behind it. He saw Chesham there and his eyes opened wider. His mouth opened as if to call out, and at that moment Chesham struck.

He pushed the door shut quickly with his shoulder and wrapped his left arm around Jake's neck, tightening it like a snake crushing its prey. Jake's powerful hands shot up and grasped Chesham's forearm, the fingers digging into the muscle in an attempt to pry the arm away from his throat. Chesham raised his right arm, the short but extremely sharp blade of his knife extending from his fist, and drove it hard into Jake's neck directly below the ear. He thrust the blade in and pushed his hand forward, severing the cowpunch's right jugular. Blood spurted from the man's neck, spraying the wall and the desk. A groan came from deep within Jake's throat, his air supply still blocked by Chesham's arm. He struggled briefly, and then his body went slack, the blood still pouring from the fatal wound in his neck. Chesham carried him forward and laid the dead man on the couch near the window. He wiped off the blade of the knife on Jake's Levi's.

He moved back to the door and opened it enough to give him a view down the hallway to the lobby. He could see the edge of the woman's shoe showing at the side of the desk. She was sitting in the chair.

'Nobody in the office,' he said, lowering his voice. 'I'm going to check the alley and have a smoke.'

She waved a hand without looking around. 'All right, then.'

He stepped into the hallway, closing the office door as he did so. With two steps, he reached the back door and went out into the alley. The rain had stopped and there was no one to be seen. He turned right and began making his way back to the yard where he had left his horse. When he reached it, he walked the horse into the alley and mounted, riding not back toward the cabin but toward Mandy Smith's café, which was only three blocks away.

He didn't notice the man emerge from the shadows of the millinery shop and begin to follow him on foot.

After Hank Chesham had left her little room behind the café, it had taken Mandy a few days before she was able to sleep soundly. She had no idea when she would see him again, although he had said it would probably be in a week or ten days. It had been five days so far, and she knew he had been busy. The burning of the Double F and the dynamiting of its well were virtually all people could talk about in the café, although no one in town had connected the events to Chesham. Apart from Mandy and a handful of people at the Rimrock, no one even knew Chesham had returned.

She took comfort in the knowledge that he hadn't been caught by Ted Flynn or his men. She knew Chesham was more than capable of taking care of himself. But there was no denying the extreme danger he placed himself in every time he moved against Flynn.

She had been asleep for a few hours when a persistent tapping on her door brought her to a wakeful state. She got up and crossed the room, where she parted the curtains. Standing there in the alley, holding his horse's reins, was Hank Chesham.

Mandy opened the door and Chesham entered the room, leaving his horse standing in the alley. They embraced and kissed before either spoke.

'Hank,' she said. 'I've been so worried.'

He smiled. 'It's nice to know that someone cares,' he said drily.

'You know I do.'

'I know that,' he said, stroking her hair. 'I'm being careful – believe me.'

'I know you are. What brings you here? I wasn't expecting you for a few more days.'

Chesham's expression lost its lightheartedness. 'I can't stay long. I just killed one of Flynn's boys at the boarding house.'

Mandy's face paled. 'Oh, God,' she said quietly.

'It was him or me,' he said simply. He unbuttoned his coat and removed the letters. 'I also found these.'

She read the words on the envelopes. 'Who is Ray Owens?' she asked. 'And why was he writing letters to Ted Flynn?'

He smiled sourly. 'Owens is the crooked judge who sent me to prison,' he replied. 'And he was paid off by Ted Flynn.'

'How do you know?'

'Read these when I leave.'

She examined the unopened letters that Chesham had sent from prison. 'Nobody ever even read these,' she said.

'Phoebe might never have even seen them,' he observed. 'Not that it makes any difference now.'

'What do you want me to do with these?'

'Keep them here – some place safe. Not that anyone will come looking for them, but you can never be too sure. They're proof that Ted Flynn has been behind all of this, from the very beginning. He saw an opportunity when I was arrested down there, and he grabbed it with both hands. He wanted Phoebe and he wanted the Rimrock – and he got them both. For a while, anyway. His day is coming.'

She nodded. 'I'll keep them for you.'

Chesham kissed her again. 'It won't be long before this will be over. I'm going to give those letters to a lawyer and see what can be done to get me my ranch back. First, though, I want to meet with Ted, just the two of us. Man to man.'

Mandy looked into Chesham's eyes, and he recognized the deep strength within her. She had already taken so many risks to help him, and she had done so fearlessly. He remembered yet again that, were it not for her, he would be dead.

'I'll see you soon – I promise,' he said.

They kissed a final time, and then Chesham crossed to the door and went out into the night.

Mandy watched him ride away down the alley, then pulled the curtain back across the window and locked the door.

Had she glanced the other way, she might have seen Al King step out the darkness, watching Chesham ride away.

CHAPTER EIGHT

Ted Flynn stopped pacing the floor of his study at the Rimrock and gazed through the window at the misty fields outside. He lifted the tumbler of brandy to his lips and noticed that his hand was shaking, ever so slightly. He swore and downed the liquor, his eyes watering from its potency. Then he splashed more brandy into the glass from the table by the window.

It had been several days since the burning of the store, and Flynn was painfully aware of the toll that his conflict with Chesham was taking on his nerves. He was trying his damndest to keep it from Phoebe, but he knew she was sensing his unease, too. The entire thing was overwhelming their lives.

Flynn had never been an early riser if he could avoid it. Yet here it was, just after dawn, and he was wide awake, pacing the floor yet again. It seemed to be all he could do, apart from drink. He had never been a big drinker, and now he found himself downing liquor before he even had his breakfast. This, too, he was trying to hide from Phoebe.

He pushed a stray tendril of hair from his forehead and glanced at the painting of Phoebe hanging above the fireplace. Everything he had done over the last five years had been for her. He had had little cause for regret until now, although his regret wasn't for any of his actions. What he regretted was not making sure that Hank Chesham had died in New Mexico. It wouldn't have been difficult to arrange. He had, however, been assured that incarceration in that hellhole of a prison down there meant that Chesham was as good as dead.

How had he gotten out of prison? Flynn had sent telegrams to Santa Fe for more information. At first he had wondered if Chesham had escaped, but the information he received in response to his queries told him that the man had been lawfully released by order of the presiding judge, Ray Owens. The late Ray Owens. The esteemed jurist whom Flynn had paid three thousand dollars to send Hank Chesham away for good.

None of it made sense, but Flynn had decided to stop trying to unravel the reasons for Chesham's freedom. The most important thing now was to track down Chesham himself and make damn good and sure he was dead. According to King and Rowland, he was as good as dead when they left him in the alley that night. Flynn had always known Chesham was a hard man, but he was proving even tougher than Flynn had ever imagined.

Flynn had known Chesham for years before the events in New Mexico. Chesham had worked off and on for Jim and Tod Flynn, Ted's father and uncle, when they had been alive. He had always been an outstanding cowpuncher, a man who understood cattle and horses and how to work on a ranch. Even then, Flynn had recognized a determination and ambition in the young man. Also, at least at that time, a certain naïveté. Chesham was the kind of man who was utterly without guile, and who interacted with others without worrying too much about whether they were as honest as he was. He seemed to accept that they were.

Those days were now past – to put it mildly. Flynn knew that he was more responsible than anyone else for the hard cynicism that characterized Chesham now. He was a changed man – a dangerous man.

Flynn had always liked Chesham until the day he learned that Phoebe was to be Hank's wife. Ted Flynn had been thinking of courting Phoebe Smith for a year before she announced her engagement to Chesham. When they had told him the good news, he had done an admirable job of feigning joy on their behalf. Inside, he had been mired in despair. He cursed himself for not pursuing her earlier. After some time passed, he finally adjusted to the idea of not having Phoebe as his own. When his father and uncle both died within a few weeks of each other, he had inherited the Double F and absorbed himself in running the ranch; it helped keep his mind off Phoebe, and it distracted him from the simmering resentment he harbored for Chesham.

When Chesham had come to him to ask for a loan, Flynn had agreed. To have Phoebe at the Rimrock, right next to the Double F, was more than he could resist. Just to be able to see her that often was irresistible to him. His loan had seemed to endear him to her, and he became a frequent guest at the Rimrock in its early days under the Cheshams.

He had helped Chesham with the things the new ranch owner didn't know – administrative things like paperwork to buy the ranch and stock, and how to distribute wages to the crew. There was nothing he couldn't teach Chesham about daily life as a rancher. The man knew everything there was to know.

Flynn would never have helped Chesham if it hadn't been for Phoebe. As time went on and he got to see her on a near-daily basis, his obsession had grown. Just riding up to the main house at the Rimrock and seeing her standing on the veranda filled him with longing. Seeing her, talking to her, hearing her laugh – these things became his reason for living. And seeing her in Hank Chesham's arms, kissing him and being his wife, deepened Flynn's private loathing for the owner of the Rimrock.

When Art Chesham had died in New Mexico and

Hank went south to settle the estate, Flynn had Phoebe all to himself. Indeed, Chesham had specifically asked his friend to look after her. He trusted Ted Flynn; he had never had a reason not to.

The arrival of the telegram informing Phoebe of her husband's arrest had come like a bolt out of the blue. Flynn had contacted some of his associates in Santa Fe, men he had come to know through his father and uncle. They had warned him that Judge Owens was a crooked jurist, and that Chesham may not receive a fair trial. Flynn had seen his opportunity and rolled the dice, not knowing if Owens would agree or not. He did.

It had all been so easy – perhaps too easy, he now thought. Because five years passed, five incredible, almost unbelievable years; years in which he acquired everything he had ever imagined and more; and then Hank Chesham reappeared, eager to take back what he felt was rightfully his, and to destroy Ted Flynn if that was necessary. He was well on his way to achieving his goal.

Don Rowland had ridden in from the hills the night before, his frigid crew with him. After searching for three solid days, they had found not the slightest hint of where Chesham might be hiding. Flynn had called off the search for the time being, adding the men to the guards who now prowled the grounds of the Rimrock.

He gulped down another mouthful of brandy and

then stiffened. In the distance, he spotted Al King riding through the gate, heading for the main house at a rapid pace. A knot tightened in Flynn's gut as he considered the implications of King's arrival. Had Chesham struck again? That seemed the only possibility.

Flynn polished off the rest of his drink and wiped his lips with his sleeve. He walked over and seated himself behind the desk. A minute passed, and then there was a knock on the door.

'Come in, Al,' Flynn said, as steadily as he could manage under the circumstances.

King entered the room and pushed the door closed before he walked over to the desk. He had already removed his hat.

'Morning, boss,' he said.

'I hope to God you've got some good news,' Flynn muttered.

'Good and bad, depending on how you look at it.'

'All right, then – let's hear it.'

'Jake's dead,' King said in a flat tone. 'Chesham killed him at the boarding house.'

Flynn was incredulous. 'How'd he get in?'

'The old lady said Jake went over to the saloon for a while. He must have been pretty sloshed. She came down from one of the rooms and found the laundry room open. Jake checked all the rooms, but Chesham was in the office. He cut Jake's throat and got out before the lady saw him.'

The color drained out of Ted Flynn's face as he heard King's words.

'Chesham was in the office?' he asked. 'You sure about that?'

'Very sure,' said King. 'We found Jake's body there on the couch.'

'Did it look like Chesham had gotten into anything?'

'Well, the top drawer of the desk was pulled out.'

'Was there anything in it?'

'No.'

Flynn rose and refilled his glass, which he carried back to the desk. He sat down without offering King a drink.

'Well, then – what's the good news?' he rasped.

'I saw Chesham leave the boarding house,' King said.

'You didn't shoot him?'

King shook his head. 'I wanted to see where he went, see if anyone was helping him. And someone is.'

Flynn raised his eyes. 'Who?' he asked harshly.

'Mandy Smith.'

'Don't be making jokes, Al,' Flynn said.

'I ain't, boss. I followed him from the alley to her café. He went into the back room and came out a few minutes later. I saw them kiss each other.'

'Christ Almighty!'

King couldn't help but be amused by Flynn's distress, although he didn't allow it to show. Flynn had never been an easy man to work for, although he compensated for this by paying his men very well. This had been especially true after he married Phoebe and acquired the Rimrock. Al King had always had a secret contempt for him. He always knew that, beneath the bravado, Flynn was a weak man.

King said: 'I'm just telling you what I saw.'

'Why didn't you follow him?' Flynn demanded, always eager to find something to criticize.

'I didn't have my horse,' King said. 'I was coming up the alley from the livery when I spotted Chesham.' With Flynn's eyes on him, he walked over to the bar and poured himself a generous glass of expensive Scotch whisky. He turned and gazed levelly at Flynn. 'Now you can hit Chesham where it hurts. You can break him. All you have to do is get your hands on Mandy Smith.'

Flynn's eyes were bleary. 'Take Mandy?'

'Well, how else are you going to make Hank Chesham listen to reason? There's something between them. They looked real close, like they're in love or something.'

'Hank and Mandy. . . .' Flynn said. 'Hard to believe.' He considered pouring himself another brandy, but then rejected the idea. He had things to consider now. 'Here's what I want you to do, Al,' he said, an element of command in his voice. 'Tonight, you need to go into town and take Mandy. You and a couple of our most reliable boys. It has to be quiet and fast.'

King nodded, knowing that he would be rewarded handsomely if the abduction came off without a hitch.

'I'll take care of it,' he said. 'Where do you want me to take her?'

'Take her to the shack at the eastern end of the Double F. Make sure none of the 'punchers see you boys bringing her there. Have the fellers you choose to take with you stand guard at the shack. I'll be there at dawn tomorrow.'

King finished his whisky and placed the glass on the table. He turned and went out of the office without another word to Ted Flynn.

Flynn heard the front door of the house close, and then almost immediately the door to his office opened again. He raised his head and a jolt of fear ran through him. Phoebe was standing in the doorway, watching him warily. He managed a half-smile.

'Hello, honey,' he said. He was worried that she had overheard his conversation with King. 'Everything all right?'

'Yes, Ted. As well as it can be at a time like this.'

After an awkward moment, Flynn asked: 'Is there anything you need?'

She walked forward and sat on the edge of the desk.

110

'I've been thinking, Ted.'

'About what?'

'About where you might find Hank.'

He raised an eyebrow, relieved that she didn't mention Mandy. 'You think you know where he might be?'

'I don't know why I hadn't thought of this before, and it might be completely wrong. . . .'

'Go on, now, dear.'

'Well, his aunt used to live in a cabin. It's south of here, in the mountains. It's very hard to find if you don't know where to look.'

Flynn rose and took his wife's hand. 'Do you know where this place is?'

'I don't think I could find the cabin. But I could show you and the men where to look. He took me there once, just before he left for New Mexico.'

'I can get Rowland and the boys saddled up in a few minutes. Are you up for a ride?'

'Yes,' said Phoebe. 'But I want to ask one thing of you, Ted. Please hear me out.'

'Anything, dear. What is it?'

'Please promise me that you won't kill Hank.'

Flynn scoffed. 'What?'

Her face was stern. 'You must promise me that you won't kill Hank, and that you won't have Don Rowland or Al King do it, either.'

'Phoebe, do you know what he has done?'

'Ted, do you know what we have done? We

111

thought he would be in prison forever, but that wasn't the case. I needed you and I have no regrets. But you have to see things his way, too. I just don't want you to kill him, Ted. I can't have that on my conscience.'

Lying came easily to Ted Flynn, but his wife's steady gaze unnerved him. He turned his head toward the window.

'You have my word.'

CHAPTER NINE

The sound of a man's voice made Mandy Smith sit bolt upright. Was it Hank, back again so soon? But then another man spoke, and she knew it wasn't Hank Chesham standing outside her door.

She pushed off her blankets and walked to her dresser. Just as she opened the top drawer to reach for her small pistol, someone tried to kick in her back door. Wood splintered and the door sagged on its hinges. Mandy screamed, and then another kick smashed the door partially open. She could see three men standing in the alley beyond.

'Go away!' she yelled, removing the pistol from the drawer.

The man in front rammed his shoulder into the door, and now it collapsed forward on to the floor of Mandy's bedroom. The man stepped in and smiled.

'You need to come with us, Miss Smith,' he said.

He took another step toward her, his arms reaching out to encircle her small frame. She raised the pistol and pulled the trigger; the bullet took him in the chest and he went down like a poled steer.

The two other men rushed her then, and the larger of the two gripped her wrist painfully, forcing her to drop the weapon.

'You shouldn't have done that,' he said, his face mottled with rage. He swung hard at her with his other hand, hitting her in the side of the head. She went limp in his arms and he carried her to the bed. As he wrapped her unconscious form in the blankets, he barked orders at his companion.

'Get a sheet and wrap up Chet,' he said. 'We'll take him back with the girl.'

The other man obeyed immediately, and they carried the two motionless forms wrapped in bed-clothes to the wagon parked in the alley behind the café. Then they climbed up into the seat and the big man flicked the reins. The wagon disappeared into the night.

Hank Chesham was awake, lying on the rickety bed in the cabin. Through the dirty window above the stove, he watched the moonlight streaming through the skeletal branches of the trees.

It had been two nights since he had found the letters at the boarding house. The contents of the letters had occupied his mind ever since, far more than the killing of the cowboy named Jake. Chesham took no pleasure in killing, but he knew that Jake would have killed him if the opportunity had presented itself.

Knowing that Ted Flynn had been behind all the suffering he had experienced in the Pile had been difficult for Chesham to comprehend. There had been more than a few times in jail when Chesham came close to death, either through illness or through a violent encounter with another inmate. There were prisoners there who would gladly kill another prisoner for shoes, or tobacco and cigarette papers, or simply to relieve the crushing tedium of daily life in prison. Chesham could scarcely believe that Flynn had been behind all that, too – that every time someone pulled a knife on him in the prison yard, it had been Flynn's fault that Chesham was even in such a position.

He thought of the unopened letters and wondered if Phoebe ever even knew that he had been writing to her. The fact that they were kept in Flynn's desk indicated that Phoebe might have thought that Chesham had abandoned her after being sent to prison. It made him wonder if, perhaps, his initial judgment of Phoebe's betrayal had been overly cynical.

However, it was the letters that answered all the important questions Chesham had had about the last five years. Why had Flynn even bothered to keep them? It didn't make sense to Chesham, particularly the decision to keep the letters from Judge Owens. Only two things could explain the decision to keep them, Chesham decided. Flynn never thought Hank Chesham would make it out of the Pile alive; and he likely took some surreptitious pleasure in having them.

Before finding the letters, he had been willing to let Flynn live, provided he signed the Rimrock back over. But now he knew that he would kill Ted Flynn – after he got the Rimrock.

Chesham had thought these things over so many times that he was weary of them. He pushed off his blanket and sat up. Through the window, a sudden movement in the trees caught his attention. When he looked again at where he had seen the movement, moonlight briefly glinted off something metal.

Instantly Chesham dove off the bed on to the dirt floor. He removed his pistol from his holster and broke it, checking the loads. He snapped it shut and reached for his rifle. It was fully loaded.

He crouched and moved past the window to the wall by the door. From this vantage point, he had a good view of most of the clearing outside, while remaining hidden from anyone in the trees. The moonlight was bright, but the area where the clearing met the forest was in darkness. He watched for several seconds, trying to discern any movements in the murky blackness. A minute passed and he almost

116

wondered if he had imagined what he had seen before.

But then some branches moved and he saw the outline of a man's hat behind the tree. Almost immediately he saw another person standing there, just behind the man who had moved the branches.

There was no doubt now. Flynn's men had found him. Only through dumb luck had he thwarted their element of surprise.

His pulse quickened as he saw one of the men move away from the trees and begin making his way carefully across the grass toward the cabin. Then another man moved into the clearing and began circling around to block the door. A third man then began to follow the first up toward the window.

Chesham thought quickly. He stood still until the two men were about five feet from the window, and then he stepped out of the darkness and raised his Navy Colt. He brought down his left hand and chopped at the hammer, sending bullets flying through the window at the men outside. The man in front took three shots to the chest, sending him hurtling backward into the man behind him. The second man's face showed panic, and he reached for his pistol just as Chesham's other bullets hit him – one in the chest, another in the neck, and the third directly in the forehead.

The gunfire was deafening in the silence of the fall night. Chesham heard the man who had circled round the cabin yell something. He dropped to the ground, reaching for his rifle. Bullets exploded through the closed door and passed over his head as the man outside fired his pistol. Chesham pointed his rifle at the door and fired once. The man outside screamed, and Chesham heard his body crash to the ground.

Chesham crawled to the door and pulled it open, his rifle ready in case the man was about to fire. He exhaled when he saw that the man was dead. He moved toward the doorway and a bullet whistled past his head, slamming into the doorjamb only inches above him. Dropping down on to his elbows, he put his rifle against his shoulder and aimed where he had seen the muzzle flash a second before. He fired, and a man in the trees leapt to his feet, clutching his chest with his left hand while trying to point his pistol at Chesham with his right. Chesham levered and fired again, taking him in the throat. The man fell back into the trees, dead before he hit the ground.

Chesham was on his feet, his eyes sweeping over the edge of the forest. A fourth bushwhacker moved in the trees, firing wildly as he fled. Chesham sent a bullet after him, paused long enough to slip on his boots, and then gave chase, gripping his rifle as he ran.

He crashed into the trees, just able to see the gunman up ahead of him. Chesham realized he was running to wherever it was that he had left his mount. Chesham pushed forward, desperate to catch up with the man.

They were running up the incline to the forested ridge on the north side of the little valley. The trees thinned and the man entered a small clearing just beneath the ridge. He turned and raised his pistol, firing directly at Chesham. The bullet grazed Chesham's left shoulder, but before he was even aware of the pain, he brought his rifle up and fired from the hip. The bullet hit the man in the left forearm, spinning him around and throwing him to the ground. The man was only down for a moment, though; in seconds, he was back on his feet, running for his life. He crossed out of the clearing into the trees as Hank Chesham narrowed the distance between them.

Chesham spotted the outlines of five horses among the trees above him. The now-injured man was making for the nearest of them. Chesham knew he wouldn't catch up with the man before the latter reached his horse. He stopped, lifted the rifle, and took careful aim at the shadowy form moving through the trees, firing where he thought his legs would be. The man's legs flew out from under him and he collapsed into the grass a few feet from his horse.

Chesham approached him slowly; he could hear the man's gasps and whimpers. He was clawing at the ground in a futile attempt to reach his mount.

Chesham halted at the edge of the trees, his rifle trained on his quarry.

'You can go ahead and stop right there,' he said. 'I got you dead to rights, pard.'

The man still had his pistol in his right hand, and he lifted it toward Chesham. Chesham fired, hitting him in the right forearm, shattering the bones. The pistol flew from the man's hand into the grass several yards away, and he rolled into a ball, clutching his arm. He now had three bullets in him. His eyes blazed at Chesham.

'You going to kill me now, Chesham?' he said.

'That depends on you,' Chesham said coldly as he approached the man. He stopped a few feet away. 'You want to die?'

'N-no. . . .'

'What's your name?'

'Rowland. Don Rowland.'

'How did you find this place?'

Rowland's chest heaved as he spoke. 'We got told about it.'

'Who told?'

'Phoebe.'

A cold fury seized Chesham. 'Phoebe?'

Rowland nodded. 'Yeah. She told Ted.'

'What's Flynn's plan?' Chesham asked.

'He doesn't . . . have one,' Rowland said, clearly in intense agony from his bullet wounds. 'He just wants you dead. You got him real scared.'

Chesham stared at Rowland for several seconds, then said: 'He's a dead man. He just doesn't know it yet.'

'Please – please. I got to get to a sawbones.'

Chesham raised the barrel of his gun and aimed it at Rowland's chest. 'You think I owe you that, you four-flushing son of a bitch? I remember you from the alley.'

'I don't want to die!'

'Maybe you should have found a different line of work, then.'

'I have some information. . . .'

'What information?'

Rowland spoke through teeth clenched from the pain. 'About your woman—'

'What?'

'Phoebe's sister.'

Chesham leaned forward. 'What about her?'

'Will you let me live?'

'Maybe. Or maybe I'll shoot you in your other leg, just to keep things interesting.'

'OK, OK,' Rowland said, lightheaded from the blood loss. 'Flynn's got Mandy.'

'Where?'

'Will you let me live?'

Chesham pointed the rifle and fired a shot in the man's uninjured leg. Rowland screamed, writhing on the ground.

'I'm only going to ask one more time,' Chesham

121

snarled. 'Where?'

'In the shack at the east side of the Double F!'

'You sure?'

Rowland nodded. 'Please—'

The rifle spat flame, the bullet entering Rowland's right eye. He fell back on to the grass and his body twitched a few times before becoming permanently still.

CHAPTER TEN

The Double F ranch was a little more than seven-hundred acres. Like the Rimrock, which it adjoined, it was dominated by a broad valley and surrounded by forested foothills. The McKenzie river was only a little over a mile away.

The shack where Ted Flynn had confined Mandy Smith was on the far eastern edge of the property, in a thicket of maple and fir trees. For years, it had been used by the Double F ranch hands, although it had been some time since anyone had slept there. It was a dirty, rundown structure with a dirt floor, a set of bunk beds, and a small wooden table and chair. There were no windows.

Mandy Smith lay on the bottom bunk, still wrapped in the blanket from her bedroom. Her head was pounding from the blow she had received. The man who had hit her was named Al; she knew this from hearing his conversation with another of

Flynn's henchmen just as they arrived at the shack. She had only been conscious for a few minutes, jostling in the back of the wagon, when they had reached their destination. Having never been to the shack before, she had no inkling of where she was.

She had feigned unconsciousness when Al King and his friend had removed her from the wagon and brought her into the shack. They deposited her on the bunk and she listened to them talk.

'She still ain't woke up, Al,' said the smaller man.

'Aw, she'll be all right,' said King.

'You hit her pretty good.'

'Well, she'd just killed Chet,' King retorted, his voice laced with annoyance. Mandy thought that he wasn't a man accustomed to being questioned. 'Should I have let her shoot you, too?'

'Nah – I ain't saying that. But if she's hurt bad you know Ted'll have a fit.'

'Let him have a fit, then. He can do his own dirty work next time if he don't like the job I'm doing for him.'

Someone lighted a lamp and placed it on the table, the wick down low. The two men stepped out into the dirt outside the shack and began smoking cheroots. Mandy kept her eyes closed, but she was seized by anxiety.

Ted Flynn, she thought. He's the one who ordered this.

She wondered if Flynn had captured Hank

124

Chesham, too. The thought filled her with dread. If Flynn got his hands on Chesham, the latter was as good as dead. She also knew that Flynn would kill her if he felt he needed to.

Had they learned about the letters she had received from Chesham? She knew there was no way that he would have told Flynn or his men about them, but somehow they had learned she was helping him. She had no idea how they had done it, but here she was, completely defenseless, in the dark both literally and figuratively.

Approaching hoofbeats drew her attention. The men out front stopped talking. The horse drew nearer and then halted outside the shack. She heard a new voice, commanding and determined – the voice of Ted Flynn.

'She here?' he asked, having offered no greetings to his men.

'She's here,' said Al King.

She heard the creak of saddle leather as Flynn dismounted. A shadow crossed the threshold and then Flynn was standing before her. She opened her eyes and stared directly at him.

'You've really done it this time, Ted,' she said, her eyes glinting in the dim light of the lamp.

'The same could be said for you,' he replied. He sat down on the table and folded his arms across his chest. 'How long have you been working with Hank Chesham?'

Her gaze was unwavering. 'Since the day you sent your men to beat him to death in that alley.'

Flynn's lips tightened. 'You sure have developed a sharp tongue, Mandy.'

'Having to talk to a yellow-bellied murderer is distasteful to me,' she said.

Without a word, Flynn was on his feet. He leaned over the bunk and slapped Mandy Smith hard across the face. Within seconds, an angry red welt in the shape of his hand began to rise on her pale skin.

'You wouldn't do that to Hank,' she said defiantly. 'Only to a woman.'

Flynn chuckled, shaking his head. 'You don't know what kind of trouble you're in, Mandy. You made the biggest mistake of your life when you decided to go all in with Chesham.'

'And you made the biggest mistake of your life when you bribed that judge to send Hank to prison. The judge had a change of heart on his deathbed. He released Hank and gave him a thousand dollars. That's how he got back to Oregon.'

Flynn's pulse was pounding visibly in a vein on his left temple. 'None of that can be proved,' he asserted.

'Yes, it can,' she countered.

'And how's that?' he asked warily.

Despite his outward confidence, Flynn was scared. Mandy could see it in his eyes, in the nervous tension in his movements. She knew at that moment that

126

Flynn's men hadn't found the letters, if they had even bothered to search her room for them.

'I have the letters. And you'll never find them.'

Flynn sneered. 'You sure about that?'

'For all you know, I've put them in the mail to Phoebe. What if she gets her hands on the mail before you do?'

A savage expression hovered over Flynn's lined features. His currant-like eyes regarded her with unalloyed hatred.

'You know, me and my boys have ways of making a woman talk,' he said, his tone strangely flat and metallic. 'There are methods I can employ that you probably couldn't imagine.'

Cold fear made the back of Mandy's neck tingle. 'I wouldn't put anything past you, Ted Flynn,' she said.

'That's wise,' he said. He stood up, still staring at her with a disconcerting sort of detachment, as if he didn't know her. She was an enemy now, and there would be no mercy for Mandy Smith. 'This can be easy, or it can be hard. The choice is yours – for now.' He called over his shoulder, 'Come on in here, Al. And bring a rope.'

The door opened a minute later and Al King entered the shack, a coiled rope in his right hand. Flynn jerked a thumb toward Mandy.

'Tie her to that chair,' he said. 'She says she ain't in the mood to talk.'

King grinned. 'She'll talk.'

127

'Hell yes, she'll talk,' said Flynn. He turned and walked out of the shack, shutting the door behind him.

Mandy's eyes met King's. His face was cold, but she could see a glint of pleasure in his expression. He kicked the chair toward the bunk on which Mandy lay. She made no attempt to move, and King's grin widened as he reached toward her. He grabbed a handful of her hair and wrenched her neck painfully, pulling her from the bed and shoving her roughly to the chair. She fell back on to it, her head throbbing.

King leaned down to tie her. She raised her hands and raked her nails down his face, scraping off flesh as she did so. King roared, and she slapped him with all the strength she could muster.

'You bitch!' he cried, raising a fist to punch her.

The door to the shack burst open and Flynn appeared in the doorway.

'Don't hit her, Al,' he said. 'Hold her arms and I'll tie her myself.'

King lowered his fist reluctantly, his face tight with barely suppressed fury. He moved around behind Mandy and grabbed her arms, holding them in place. Flynn stepped forward and took the rope. He knelt before Mandy and reached out to tie her legs to the chair. At that moment, she kicked him hard in the nose and mouth with her bare right foot.

Blood spurted from Flynn's nose as he fell backward on to the floor. He reached up and felt his face, regarding the blood that came away on his fingers with disbelief. He pushed himself to his feet and slapped Mandy Smith across the face. She gasped, her head spinning.

'Clem!' Flynn called. 'Come on in here and hold this bitch's legs. Now!'

Clem came in immediately and obeyed Flynn's command. This time, Mandy didn't try to kick. Flynn had her securely tied within ninety seconds. He stood back up and removed a handkerchief from his shirt pocket. He held it against his bloody nose and swollen lips.

'You two go back out,' he said. 'This is between me and her.'

The men went out of the shack, pulling the door closed. Mandy raised her head and regarded Flynn. She said nothing.

He finished staunching the blood flow and tossed the handkerchief on to the table. His right hand disappeared into the inside pocket of his coat and Mandy's eyes widened when it emerged.

In it was a short, pearl-handled knife. Flynn tested the edge of it against the pad of his thumb and then stared at Mandy, a smile tugging at the corner of his mouth.

When he spoke, his voice was oily and controlled.

'Where are those letters, Mandy? You shouldn't have told me Hank gave them to you. I figured he'd squirreled them away himself, but no – he enlisted his little lady friend to hide them. So where did you put them?'

'Why do you want them so badly, Ted? Aren't you an honorable man?'

'I have my reasons for the things I've done. I don't need to explain them to you.'

'You might have to explain them to Phoebe someday,' said Mandy. 'Have you ever thought of that?'

Flynn smirked. 'I won't be needing to explain anything to Phoebe, either.'

'If she knew the things you've done—'

'Phoebe is a very happy woman now, Mandy,' Flynn said evenly. 'She has a life beyond anything she ever dreamed of before. She wouldn't have this life if it weren't for me. Hank Chesham would never have given it to her.'

'Hank is a decent man. He's not a liar and a cheat. He doesn't bribe judges to destroy other people's lives and take what's rightfully theirs.'

Flynn's mouth was a thin line as he glared at her. For a moment she thought he was going to hit her again.

'Hank wouldn't have been able to buy the Rimrock if I hadn't helped him out. He could bust broncs and herd cattle, but he didn't know diddly about making money.'

Mandy's voice dripped with disdain. 'So that's how you justify sending him to prison and taking his wife

130

and land?'

'Hank was in over his head. Way over his head. He would have lost everything anyway, and ruined Phoebe in the process. Whether you believe it or not, everything I've done has been for her. I love your sister, Mandy. If you love her, you'll be glad that I did what I did.' He raised the knife and the blade glinted in the lantern light. 'Let's not forget what we were talking about. The letters, Mandy. You know where they are. There's been too much bloodshed already. Those letters get into the wrong hands and you will destroy Phoebe's life, too. Do you want to be responsible for that?'

'Phoebe has already made her choice, and so have you.'

Flynn's face hardened. 'Suit yourself,' he said. 'I'm through talking.'

He moved closer to her, twirling the blade in his fingers. Mandy pulled herself back in her chair instinctively as his shadow fell across her. He reached out and stroked her hair.

'You've always had pretty hair, Mandy,' he said soothingly. 'Just like your sister. You're proud of it, aren't you?' He grinned when she didn't answer. 'Of course you are. And who can blame you?'

He gripped a large tuft of her lustrous hair and hacked at it with the knife. She cried out as he dropped a handful of hair on to the dirt floor. He laughed and took another handful, sawing at it close

131

to her scalp, and then stepped back and held it up in front of her face.

'Hair'll grow back,' he said. 'Your fingers won't. You get what I'm saying or do you still want to play dumb?'

Chesham returned to his cabin and dressed quickly. He strapped on his gun belt and reloaded his pistol. He replaced the rounds he had used in the rifle and walked out to the lean-to, stepping over the body of one of Flynn's men as he brought his horse out and saddled it.

He knew exactly where the shack on the east end of the Double F was. He had been there many times in the past; he had even slept there on a few occasions when he had spent a summer working for Ted Flynn's father. It was in a secluded spot, surrounded by trees. It would be ideal for holding someone hostage without attracting any attention.

Chesham stopped near the bodies of the two men he had killed through the window. He knelt and took their pistols, which he shoved into the waistband of his pants. He put a foot in a stirrup and climbed into leather.

He figured it would take him two hours to reach the shack. He considered the best way to approach it, since he knew there would be men surrounding it. He decided to circle around the Double F and leave his horse in the trees just south of the shack.

After nearly a half an hour of riding, Chesham was heeling his sorrel up a steep, forested incline when the animal whickered, spooked by something up ahead. Chesham neck-reined the horse to the right, moving into the shelter of the trees. He alighted and tied the reins to a large branch of a fir tree. Then he removed the rifle from the scabbard on the saddle and crouched, looking toward the trees further up the incline.

His horse's keen senses had likely saved his life. A man on a horse emerged through the trees up above and began to make his way down toward Chesham's position. A few seconds later, he was followed by another rider.

Chesham drew his pistol and waited among the thick branches for the men to pass by. They did so without noticing his presence. Just as the second man passed him, he stepped out behind them and leveled his weapon.

'Hold it right there, gents,' he said. Both men pulled reins and looked back at him. 'Either one of you tries anything funny and you'll both be eating lead. Got it?'

The men nodded, and the man closest to Chesham said: 'You Hank Chesham?'

'That's my name. Ted Flynn send you to help out your pards?' They were silent, not sure if they should answer the question. Chesham thumbed back the hammer on his Colt in order to make them more loquacious. 'Did he?' he demanded loudly.

'Yeah,' the man in front replied. 'We work for Flynn.'

'Well, unless you want to end up like the five other sidewinders he sent out here, you'll do as I tell you. You hear me?'

The men mumbled fearful agreement, both clearly stunned to know that this stranger holding the pistol on them had killed five of their allies.

'What you want us to do, mister?' the man in front asked.

'You're both going to pull those rifles out of the scabbards and toss them on the ground. Pronto.' They obeyed, the rifles making muffled thuds in the grass. 'Good,' Chesham continued. 'Now draw those pistols and do the same. And like I said – you try anything cute and I'll blast your asses straight out of those saddles.' He pointed the muzzle of his pistol at the man nearest him. 'You first.'

The man pulled back the side of his coat and gripped the butt of his .44. He slowly withdrew it from the holster, and then suddenly he hipped in the saddle and raised the gun toward Chesham in a fast, desperate move.

Chesham triggered a round into the man's neck. He toppled out of the saddle and the other rider yanked the reins on his horse and dug spurs into its flanks, sending it into a panicked run across the trail into the woods. Chesham fired a shot just as the man entered the trees. He narrowly missed him.

'Goddamn it!' he grated as he ran back and untied his own horse.

He could hear the man riding through the trees up the rise and knew precisely where he was headed – straight back to Ted Flynn.

Chesham brought his mount to the trail and leapt into the saddle. He drove the animal up the trail, leaving the dead man on the ground without a second glance. He hoped to catch up to the rider.

As he crested the rise, he could see the dark shapes of the man and his horse up ahead on the narrow trail. The man had cut out of the trees and was racing at a full gallop. Chesham spurred his horse to a faster pace, glad that the animal was rested, unlike the horse up ahead. The trail was only five or six paces wide and twisted its way through a long gully. Trees lined both sides.

Slowly but steadily, Chesham gained on the rider in front of him. He could see the man turn around and look back every hundred yards or so. Closer and closer came Chesham, and the man looked back once more, losing his balance as he did so. He was hurled from the saddle into the brush and lay there for a moment as Chesham slowed his horse and approached, his Colt already in hand.

'Stand up and give me your pistol,' Chesham said.

The man rose, his face drawn. His hand shook as he carefully removed his gun from its holster and held it out, handle first, to Chesham, who leaned down and grabbed it. The man gaped at him, not sure what would happen next.

A sick feeling filled Hank Chesham. He'd done more killing since returning to Oregon than he ever imagined he would have to do in his life; and he hadn't returned wanting to kill anyone to begin with. He knew that tonight he would have to kill some more. This man, however, was no longer a threat to him or to Mandy Smith. He broke the pistol open and dumped the cartridges on to the ground before raising his arm and throwing the weapon far off into the darkness of the forest.

'You'll have a long walk back,' said Chesham. 'You might consider finding a new employer.'

'I'll do that,' the man said in a tremulous voice. 'Thanks for letting me live.'

Chesham stared at him for a moment.

'Go to hell,' he said, before spurring his mount down the trail.

CHAPTER ELEVEN

Phoebe Flynn stood near a pillar on the veranda of the Rimrock's main house. She wore a green checked dress, her hair piled in a bun atop her head. Her eyes gazed down the long, straight road that led from the front gate to the house. She could just make out the wrought iron ornamentation on the gate, and the trees that swayed gently in the breeze beyond.

She wondered where her husband was. He was like a different man now – no longer the self-assured protector he had been when Hank had left for New Mexico and been sent to prison. At that time, Flynn had stepped in and promised to take care of everything. And he had. She knew nothing about running the ranch or handling its finances, and he had taken over both tasks and succeeded beyond her expectations. She had come to trust him and then, when it became apparent that Hank wasn't coming back, to like and then love him.

He had promised to look into Hank's case and see if anything could be done to have him released. He had even corresponded with the judge. When he told her that the evidence against Hank was very strong and a conviction more than likely, she felt as if her entire life had collapsed around her. She felt helpless and alone.

'Why would Hank rob a stage, Ted?' she had asked tearfully. 'I don't understand it. He'd just inherited all that money from his brother.'

Flynn spread his hands, a mournful expression on his face. 'I don't know, Phoebe. I really don't. The only thing I can think is that perhaps he wanted to pay off the entire ranch in one payment, and still have enough money to buy all the cattle he said he was going to get. He owed me money, too, remember.' He shook his head. 'I think maybe he got in over his head. Got a little too ambitious, a little too quick. That Judge Owens down in Santa Fe has a sterling reputation, Phoebe. I've talked to some of my business associates down there and they all say the same thing – if Ray Owens says Ted did it, then that's the truth.'

Not long after that conversation, things changed between Phoebe Chesham and Ted Flynn. He had been so generous and sympathetic. She had heard that the prison where Hank had been sent was so horrific that a twenty-year sentence almost surely meant that he would die there. Hearing that, she knew in her heart that Hank would never come back to her. Besides, would she really want to be reunited with him? The thought that he had robbed a stage coach was disgraceful to her, and she had felt shame, although Flynn had assured her that no one would judge her harshly for her husband's actions.

So, within a year of Hank Chesham's departure, she had annulled their marriage on the grounds of mental distress and abandonment. Shortly there-after, she had become Mrs Phoebe Flynn. The years that followed had been fulfilling, as had her rela-tionship with her new husband. Eventually she found herself more or less forgetting about Hank entirely. Whatever feelings of guilt once stirred within her had evaporated.

The union of the Double F and the Rimrock had made her the prominent woman she had always aspired and, in her view, deserved to be. She was treated with respect by everyone – no longer was she merely the daughter of an elderly café owner. She was the wife of one of the wealthiest ranchers in the southern Willamette Valley – and the wealth of the Flynns seemed destined only to grow with each passing year.

Phoebe could afford to be generous now, were she so inclined. Sometimes she was. She paid off her father's debts when he died, which allowed her sister to keep the café and the building in which it was housed. She knew that Mandy appreciated that gesture, and it pleased her that the news had quickly spread through town, largely quelling whatever unpleasant rumors had sprang up in the wake of her marriage to Ted Flynn, who was, she knew, far more respected than he was liked.

The return of Hank had torn her world asunder. She was assailed by feelings of remorse for her actions when he had been imprisoned. She couldn't deny now that she had been more concerned with her own survival and future lifestyle than she had been about Hank's fate. She wondered at the decisions she had made, and about the way in which she had shifted her allegiance to Ted Flynn. These were feelings and thoughts that she could suppress before, but not now. She had seen the look in Hank's eyes the day he rode into the yard after so many years away. It was as if he had looked right through her and been disgusted by what he had seen.

Flynn's subsequent behavior had done little to reassure her. He had become withdrawn and anxious. He was drinking more than he ever had before. Despite his assurances, she was haunted by the idea that he would kill Hank if he got the chance – a thought that was unbearable to her. She hoped that by giving him the location of the cabin where Hank might be holed up, she would also force him to turn Hank over to the sheriff. She couldn't think of any other way to end the dispute between the two men without one of them killing the other.

When Hank had disappeared almost immediately after returning home, she thought maybe Flynn had murdered him. The attacks on her husband's men and property had shown this not to be so. Instead, it had only caused more trepidation and uneasiness in Phoebe's mind.

The wind blew, rustling the bare branches of the maple tree in the yard. It was well after midnight and she had long since expected Ted to return by now. His absence worried her, as most things did these days.

She heard the sound of men's voices on the far side of the veranda, beyond the bushes. Some of the armed guards that her husband now employed to protect the Rimrock. She turned and walked in their direction, her bare feet nearly silent on the stone floor beneath her.

Perhaps they knew where Ted was, she thought. He certainly seemed to talk to them more than he did to her these days.

Phoebe stopped at the edge of the veranda. The men were obscured by a large, neatly trimmed hedge. She opened her mouth to speak, but something about their conversation caused her to listen rather than talk to them.

'So you heard what Al told us earlier?'

'I wasn't there, but Clem told me about it when I

came in. He's really going to take the lady from the café?'

'Yep.'

'Why?'

'Because the boss told him to.'

'What the hell did she do? She's the sister to his missus.'

'Well, she's been helping Chesham.'

'How you know that?'

'Al saw them together, after Chesham killed Jake.'

'I'll be damned.'

'The boss ain't playing nice anymore. Not after what Chesham done.'

Her hand clasped over her mouth, Phoebe Flynn backed away from the voices. Her mind could barely acknowledge what she had heard.

Hank and Mandy were working together. How had things come to this? Were they in love? Was she helping Hank wage his war of attrition against her husband?

She walked to a pillar and leaned against it, worried her knees were going to buckle. A deep, sickening feeling of dread filled her. Al King was 'taking' Mandy? She wondered if this meant Ted was going to use Mandy as bait to lure Hank into a trap. Or perhaps—

No, she thought. Ted wouldn't do that. He wasn't that sort of man. He could never kill his wife's sister. Hank, yes – conceivably. But not Mandy.

Phoebe put her hands over her eyes and tried to control her emotions. She stood there on the veranda for another minute, and then she turned and walked into the house, a new sense of determination in her step.

There were still two hours left before dawn as Hank Chesham concluded his ride. He had ridden around the Double F, staying south of the ranch among the forests and foothills as he made his way east. He halted at last and assessed his position, and then he moved north toward the shack. He stayed off the trails to avoid running into any more of Flynn's riders. The mission at hand called for stealth.

He drew reins in a dense cluster of firs about a quarter of a mile from the cabin. The full moon cast its pale light through shifting clouds. The air was crisp and the temperature had dropped to the point that Chesham could see his breath when he exhaled. As he sat his horse, an owl hooted from somewhere in the trees to his right. He listened for any sounds of movement in the darkness, but heard nothing.

He dismounted and picketed his horse. He removed his rifle from the scabbard and began walking in the direction of the shack. He was careful about where he placed his feet, not wanting to break a branch and reveal his position, or lose his footing and fall with the same result. He knew Flynn would have men on guard, although he wondered if there wouldn't be too many of them since so many had ridden out to kill him at the cabin.

Chesham took his time. He didn't lack firepower, with his rifle, his Navy Colt, and two of the dead men's pistols in his waist band. He also had his boot knife, which was honed razor-sharp.

A few dozen yards ahead, he could see the trees thinning out. He knew he was getting close to the shack. He had seen no sign of any guards so far. He continued forward, more cautious than ever, and then suddenly stopped dead in his tracks.

Somewhere further on, a man coughed loudly. Then a few more coughs followed, suppressed this time. Then Chesham heard the person clear his throat and spit.

He pinpointed the sound as coming from the trees surrounding the yard of the shack. The man was standing up ahead, a little to Chesham's right. So he had found the first of Flynn's men. Again, he wondered how many others were out here, invisible in the dark forest.

He moved forward, making almost no sound. He stopped again about ten feet behind the man, who was now leaning with his shoulder against a tree, looking in the opposite direction from Chesham. Chesham continued his approach, thankful that there were very few branches on the patch of ground that separated him from the guard. Wet pine needles made no sound under his boots. He was five feet from the man when the latter turned and put his back against the tree. Chesham saw that he had a knife in his hand and was using the blade to trim a callus on the palm of his other hand. Slowly the man raised his head, as if he had just become aware that he wasn't alone. He turned his head to the left and saw Chesham standing close by. It took a few seconds for him to realize what was happening, but when Chesham moved toward him, he swiped his knife outward, cutting a deep trough across Chesham's chest and ripping his flannel shirt.

He swiped again, this time aiming for the throat, but Chesham leaned back and avoided the blade. He grabbed the man's arm and pulled him in close. The man struggled to free himself, but Chesham was too strong. He attempted to stab at him again. Chesham smashed the barrel of his big Navy Colt across the man's temple and the guard immediately collapsed on to the wet ground.

He wondered briefly what to do with him. He wasn't going to strangle an unconscious man to death, despite the fact that the man had tried to kill him. He tossed the knife into the trees, and then dragged the heavy guard further back into the woods, where he dropped him beneath a skeletal birch. He removed the man's pistol and hid it beneath a large rock several yards away. Then he made his way back to the rim of trees that surrounded the shack.

145

Through gaps in the boards of the decades-old structure, he could see light from a lantern inside. He swept his eyes around the shadows of the trees, trying to discern the presence of any other guards. He waited for nearly ten minutes until he decided to move in on the shack. There didn't seem to be any more men lurking in the darkness.

Chesham had just taken a single step forward when the door to the shack abruptly opened and Ted Flynn stepped out into the square of light that now lay in the yard. He took a few steps out of the shack, looking toward the dark forest. Chesham moved back among the branches of a large nearby fir, his eyes riveted on Flynn.

From his position, he could just see into the shack, but all he saw was the shadow of the bunk beds on the back wall. He couldn't see the beds themselves, or anything else inside. He couldn't tell if Mandy was there or not.

He watched as Flynn removed a cheroot from his shirt pocket and lighted it, cupping his hand around the match. Once he got it going, Flynn shook out the match and tossed it into the grass. He clenched his teeth on the cheroot, puffing slowly, his mind clearly at work. Chesham wondered what he was thinking. Given the scarcity of guards Flynn had chosen to post around the shack, it was evident that he had confidence in the men he had sent out to kill Chesham at the cabin. If that were the case, then what did he now want with Mandy? There was nothing more for Flynn to fear if Chesham were dead. He had no reason to do anything to Mandy now.

Was Flynn unhinged to the point where he would want to take revenge on Mandy even if he thought Hank Chesham had been killed? Chesham considered this as his eyes raked over the figure standing in the yard, casually smoking a cheroot.

Yes, thought Chesham. Flynn was that far gone. The man had no boundaries anymore, if he ever had any. He would do anything to destroy those who opposed him, or who stood in the way of what he wanted.

Chesham wondered if he would be willing to kill Phoebe herself if it came down to it. He wouldn't put it past Flynn – not anymore.

Flynn turned and strode back into the shack, slamming the door behind him. A few moments passed, and then Chesham heard a woman scream. He drew his pistol and ran across the yard to the shack.

CHAPTER TWELVE

The scream came again as Chesham reached the door of the shack. He knew it was Mandy's voice.

He drew his Navy Colt with his right hand and used his left to pull one of the pistols from his waistband. He thumbed back the hammers on both guns and kicked in the door of the shack. It flew off its hinges and crashed on to the floor.

Chesham stepped through the doorway. The scene before him shocked him as few things had in his life.

Mandy Smith was roped to a chair between the bunk beds and the table. Her hair had been crudely chopped short, with bits sticking out in uneven tufts around her scalp. The upper half of her nightgown had been cut away, revealing her bare breasts. There was a multitude of small, shallow cuts on her shoulders and arms, and another down her left cheek. She was almost completely unrecognizable.

148

Flynn was standing behind her, holding the knife. Blood was smeared across its short, sharp blade. His eyes bulged as he looked at the man across the room.

'Chesham!' he spat.

Hank Chesham raised his pistol and fired at Flynn. The bullet entered the man's right shoulder, exiting through his back and lodging in the wall behind him. Flynn screamed, gripping his shoulder and falling back against the wall. The knife fell from his fingers. Chesham raised the other pistol and leveled it at him.

'You best step away from her, Ted,' he said. 'The next bullet's going through your head. If you're lucky.' Flynn hesitated for a moment before obeying Chesham. He moved over to the table and leaned against it. 'Now pull your pistol and throw it on the bunk.'

Flynn reached across with his left hand, lifted his pistol from the holster, and tossed it past Mandy on to the bed.

Chesham slipped his left-hand pistol back into his waistband and picked up Flynn's knife. He cut the rope from Mandy's ankles and then from around her arms. He lifted her from the chair. She began to sob uncontrollably, moving toward a state of hysteria. Chesham held her against him and she buried her face in his chest, oblivious to the wound there. He still kept his Colt on Flynn, whose cheek was twitching again like it had on the day Chesham returned to the Rimrock.

'You are one sick son of a bitch,' Chesham said. 'This is the end of the road for you.' His eyes had a deadly glint in them as he regarded the man who had destroyed his life. He ripped Mandy's blanket off the bunk and wrapped it around her. 'What do you think Phoebe will think when she learns the truth about you and everything you've done, even to her own sister?'

'Phoebe will never come back to you,' Flynn said.

Chesham scoffed. 'I ain't interested in Phoebe, Teddie boy. She laid down with a dog and now she's got fleas. That's her problem. But you're still interested in Phoebe, ain't you?' Flynn lowered his eyes to the dirt floor. 'She's going to have a whole new view of her loving husband.'

'Just kill me,' Flynn said. He seemed to be physically shrinking under Chesham's words. 'Kill me. I don't have anything to live for now.'

'Oh, believe me, Ted – I'm going to kill you. You can bet on that.'

'I should have had you killed years ago,' Flynn muttered. 'I should have paid off a guard and had you taken care of.'

Chesham grinned humorlessly. 'Yeah, that would have been a good idea, Ted. The problem is you were never as smart as you think you are. You're nothing but a four-flushing coward. You've never earned anything that you have, not in your entire life.

150

Everything came to you from others – your pa, your uncle. Then you paid off that judge and took Phoebe and the Rimrock from me. You're a taker, not a doer. You always were. That's why you failed.'

'You don't even know what you're talking about,' said Flynn in a defeated tone.

'Yes, I do. Now I'm taking you and Mandy over to the Rimrock and we're all going to have a little talk with Phoebe.' Chesham looked toward Mandy, who sat wrapped in the blanket. She seemed to be staring into the distance, but upon hearing Chesham's words she raised her head. 'Mandy, are you up to that?'

She nodded slowly. 'I'm up to it.'

A third man's voice suddenly boomed into the shack. 'I wouldn't get too far ahead of myself if I were you, Chesham.'

Chesham pivoted toward the door, but Al King's Remington pistol was already pointed at his head.

'Drop the gun,' King said, thumbing back the hammer. 'Now.' Chesham let his Navy Colt tumble from his fingers on to the dirt floor. King smiled. 'The others, too.' Chesham removed the two other pistols from the waist of his pants and they joined the Navy Colt.

'Where the hell you been?' Flynn cried.

King shifted his glance to his employer. 'Shut the hell up, you useless chickenshit.' Flynn's face colored as he struggled to understand the dynamics of the situation. 'I found Chesham's horse and it took me a while to get back. You should be licking my boots for saving your life.'

Flynn seemed about to say something, but refrained. What little dignity he had left before King entered the shack was now completely gone. King looked back at Chesham, and then his eyes fell upon Mandy Smith, who seemed barely to have noticed his entrance.

'Good God, Ted,' King said, shaking his head. 'You did that to her?'

Chesham realized that King, despite being a murderer, was genuinely shocked by the state of the woman on the bunk.

'Defenseless women are the only ones Ted Flynn feels comfortable fighting,' he said.

King exhaled sharply. 'Yeah, well, I'm done with all this.' He glanced back at Flynn. 'Or almost done, I should say.'

Flynn started. 'What's that supposed to mean?' he asked, clearly frightened of the answer he might receive.

'We're going to take a little trip,' King explained, addressing all three. 'We're going over to the Rimrock. You're going to open that big safe of yours, Ted, and give me some well-earned restitution for stopping Hank Chesham from killing you. Then I'm going to hit the trail and let y'all sort this out between yourselves.'

'You must be joking!' Flynn exclaimed.

'Am I?' King asked sardonically. 'Well, then, I'll just step back out and let Chesham pick up where he left off.'

'No!'

'I didn't think so.' King took a step back, waving his gun toward the doorway. 'Now come on out, all of you. Chesham first, then Flynn. I'll bring the woman.'

Recognizing that there was no alternative, Chesham moved past King and went out into the yard. Flynn followed him, keeping his distance. King walked out with Mandy before him, his pistol pressed into her back.

'You try anything, Chesham, and I'll kill her first. Don't think I won't.'

'I know you would,' Chesham said.

'Good. Now mount up and we'll head out.'

King had brought Chesham's horse and tied it to a tree on the edge of the woods. Flynn's horse was picketed nearby.

'What about her?' Chesham asked, nodding toward Mandy.

'She rides with me,' King said coolly.

As Chesham and Flynn mounted their horses, King pushed Mandy up into his saddle. He climbed up and sat behind her, reaching around her to take the reins.

'You two ride out first,' he said to Chesham and Flynn. 'We'll bring up the rear. Either one of you tries to make a run for it and I'll shoot you down before you make ten paces. Now git!'

Dawn was creeping across the heavens as they rode out of the yard down the rutted trail toward the main road that led eventually to Springfield and then Eugene. They reached the road and turned left. They rode at an easy pace, King watching the two riders in front of him like a hawk. A cold drizzle began to fall from the lightening sky.

Chesham wondered what King's plan was. Was he telling the truth when he said he would take Flynn's money and leave? It was possible. There was no question that King loathed Ted Flynn, for whatever reasons. Perhaps he had been planning something like this for a long time; perhaps he simply saw an opportunity when he returned to the shack and found it too much to resist.

It took just over twenty minutes to reach the gate to the Rimrock. They passed through it, maintaining the same unhurried gait. The men in the wide pastures stopped and stared at them. Flynn had undone a few buttons on his shirt and tucked his right arm into it. The wound in his shoulder appeared to have paralyzed it. He kept his gaze fixed firmly ahead, as did Chesham, who rode a few yards behind his nemesis.

They drew reins near the hitching post in front of the veranda. They tied their horses, and King removed a large cloth sack from his right saddle-bag.

The two guards who had been on duty since the previous evening walked around from the back of the house, their hands on the butts of their pistols.

'What the hell?' asked the older guard, a white-haired man in his sixties. 'You want us to draw, boss?'

'Shut up,' King said. 'Either of you clear leather and Flynn will be tasting lead. Savvy?'

'Listen to him!' Flynn said, a shiny layer of sweat across his face.

The guards nodded.

'Now throw those guns in the bushes – both of you,' King said.

'What the hell is going on, Al?' asked the younger guard.

'Stop your damn palavering and do as you're told,' King retorted. 'This ain't none of your concern, hear?'

'Sure, Al. Sorry for asking.'

The guards threw their pistols into the bushes near the veranda steps.

'Now go up on the porch and take a seat on that bench. Like I said, don't do anything stupid. This ain't your business, so it ain't worth dying over.' King looked to Chesham. 'You go in first, then Flynn. Go into the office.'

Chesham climbed the steps and went into the foyer of the house. He walked to the office, Flynn not far behind him. The maid came down the hallway as King, still holding his pistol in Mandy Smith's back, walked to the office door.

'Mrs Flynn is asleep right now,' she said, not seeing the gun behind Mandy. She sensed something was very wrong. 'Should I wake her up?'

'No,' King answered. 'Go back to the kitchen and keep your damn mouth shut.'

The elderly woman pursed her lips and turned back the way she had come. King pushed Mandy into the office and followed her in, closing the door quietly. Chesham was standing near the window, Flynn in front of the desk.

'Ted, you know where the safe is. Open it up and make it quick.'

Flynn's jaw was clenched as he walked slowly over to the large painting of Phoebe above the fireplace. He reached up with his left hand and the frame swung outward on a hinge, revealing the safe hidden behind it, built into the fireplace. He had had it put in shortly after marrying Phoebe.

'How much you got in there, Ted?' asked King.

'About ten thousand,' Flynn replied hoarsely, his fingers on the dial of the safe.

'Nice. Now get going.'

Flynn turned the dial, first left, then right, then left again. When he was done, he twisted the handle and pulled open the door. Both King and Chesham craned their necks to see inside. Mandy was indifferent, staring absently out the window.

Inside the safe were several tied bags containing

156

coins. There were also several neat stacks of paper money, bound with paper slips from the bank.

A wicked grin spread across Al King's face. He tossed his sack on to the desk a few feet from Flynn.

'Fill it,' he said.

Flynn glanced back into the safe. 'All of it?' he asked.

'Hell yes, all of it. You got water on the brain?'

Flynn turned and grabbed the first two stacks of cash. He carried them over to the desk and placed them in the sack. He repeated the process three times before he got to the bags of coins. He carried the first two over, then the second pair, leaving only one bag left in the safe.

King was growing impatient. 'Hurry the hell up!' he said.

Flynn turned to the safe and reached for the sack. When he turned back, the sack was still in the safe, but a .41 derringer was in his left hand.

Chesham yelled: 'Mandy, get down!'

The woman fell forward, partly pushed by King, whose pistol was turning toward Flynn.

'Better luck next time, Al,' Flynn said.

He fired the first shot, the bullet hitting King dead center in the chest. King gasped, dropping his pistol. He grabbed his chest, trying to breathe, and then his legs gave way and he crumpled on to the carpet.

Chesham took a step toward King's pistol, but Flynn trained the derringer on him. 'Stop!' he cried.

'Not another step, Hank. I still have another bullet left.'

Chesham froze, looking from Mandy to Flynn.

'My, my,' Flynn sneered. 'How the tables have turned!' He laughed – a strange, maniacal cackle. 'You thought you were all set, didn't you? Kind of like how I felt when I sent you to jail and married Phoebe. My plan didn't work out the way I thought it would. Now it looks like yours didn't either.'

'Ted, what's happened?'

All three turned and glanced to the open doorway. Phoebe Flynn stood there, looking remarkably frail. A heavy shawl was wrapped over her shoulders. Her sunken eyes were riveted on her husband.

'Phoebe,' Flynn said nervously. 'My darling. It's all over now. Al tried to rob me, but I killed him. And here's Hank. He can't do any more damage now. I was going to take him into town and turn him over to the sheriff.'

Phoebe looked at the open safe, then down to Al King's body. A pool of blood was slowly spreading on the rug around the dead man. Her gaze shifted to Chesham before settling on her sister.

'What happened to Mandy?' she asked. 'Who did this?'

'He did,' Chesham said, pointing at Ted Flynn. 'He'd have killed her, too. He's lost his damn mind.'

'That's a lie!' Flynn yelled. He looked at Phoebe. 'Al did it. If I hadn't come along, he'd have cut her throat. He wanted to use her to get to the money.'

Phoebe blinked, unsure of herself. 'Who did this, Mandy?' she asked.

Mandy Smith's voice was soft, but it seemed to fill the entire room.

'Ted did it.'

Desperation consumed Flynn. 'She's not in her right mind, Phoebe!'

'He's lying,' said Chesham. 'He slashed her over and over again. Then he was going to kill her if she didn't reveal where she'd hidden the letters.'

'What letters?'

'The letters that proved that he bribed a judge to have me put in prison. Along with the letters I wrote to you from jail that he hid from you.'

'Lies!' Flynn cried, nearly in tears now. 'Phoebe, I love you. I would never deceive you. You're my whole world!'

'Your whole world is a lie,' said Chesham in a chilly tone.

'Damn you!' Flynn screamed, pulling back the hammer on his derringer. He extended his arm and began to squeeze the trigger.

The sound of a gunshot exploded in the room and Chesham winced, waiting for the pain to come. But instead it was Ted Flynn who groaned with pain, a hole having formed in his abdomen from which blood streamed, dripping down the left leg of his pants.

Chesham looked at Phoebe. She had parted her

shawl and held a pistol in her hand. Smoke drifted up from the muzzle.

'Phoebe!' Flynn rasped. 'Why?'

'You're evil, Ted,' she responded. 'And you've hurt enough people.'

Flynn looked back at Chesham. 'You!' he said, his voice faltering. 'You. . . .'

He pointed the derringer and prepared to shoot Chesham, a last act of defiance before his death. Another shot erupted from Phoebe Flynn's pistol. It hit her husband in the chest, and he stumbled backward into the fireplace, dropping his derringer. He slid down the bricks and landed in a sitting position. A rattling sound came from his throat and then his head fell forward. He didn't move again.

Mandy rose and walked to Chesham. He put his arm around her and held her close. Neither spoke.

Phoebe threw her pistol on to the rug beside Al King's body. When she spoke, her voice was controlled.

'Let's go into town,' she said. 'We'll need to see the judge before I can sign the ranch back over to you.'

She turned and walked out of the office.

Holding a protective arm around Mandy, Chesham led her to the door, and to the new life they would now share together.